Addicted

S. Nelson

Addicted/ S.Nelson. -- 1st edition

ISBN-13: 978-1512084535
ISBN-10: 1512084530

This book is dedicated to all of the wonderful bloggers out there who tirelessly work to promote authors. I honestly don't know where most of us would be without your love and support. I'll be forever grateful for the amazing people I've met along my journey.

Acknowledgements

Thank you to my husband for being patient with me as I released one book after another, spending countless hours locked away in my office. Thank you for giving me the time I needed to get these characters out of my head and onto paper. I love you!

A huge thank you to my family and friends for your continued love and support. I don't know what I would do without you!

To the ladies at Hot Tree Editing, I can't say enough great things about you. You continue to amaze me and I can't wait until our next project together. You have been truly fantastic!

I would also like to thank Clarise at CT Cover Creations. Your work speaks for itself. I'm absolutely thrilled with this book cover. It's beyond gorgeous!

To Beth, Nicole and Renee, my new Beta team. You were the first to read Addicted and you allowed me to breathe a little easier with your wonderful feedback on Alek and Sara's story. I promise I'll get you Shattered very soon. I love you ladies!

To my other Beta readers, the kind words you've shared with me about Addicted mean more to me than you could ever know. Thank you so much for your support and I promise you'll find out what happens next for Alek and Sara very soon.

And last but not least, I would like to thank you, the reader. I hope you enjoy this book half as much as I enjoyed writing it.

Prologue

Sara

Holy Hell! What in God's name happened?

Cotton mouth, throbbing temples and a nauseous stomach had me instantly regretting the previous night. Rolling onto my stomach, I put more pressure on my bladder than I'd wanted. I was desperately trying to get into a more comfortable position but the only thing I managed to do was aggravate my poor little organ, so full I thought I was going to have an accident. Deciding I didn't want a mess to clean up, I turned over and slowly swung my legs off the side of the mattress, my head spinning the moment I sat upright. I took a minute before standing up, desperately hoping the feeling wouldn't last all day.

Carefully walking around my bed, I ventured into the short hallway. I slowly made my way toward the bathroom, my eyes adjusting to the darkness with every step. After I'd taken care of business, I quickly washed my hands and headed back to my room, still a little groggy.

It was super-early, or super-late; whichever way you wanted to look at it.

As I pushed my bedroom door open wider, I saw the bright green light of the alarm clock. 4:22 am. *I'm going with super-early.* I didn't feel like walking all the way around only to climb onto my side of the mattress. Actually, there was only me, so I wasn't sure why I even deemed the left side as *my* side. Either way, I didn't want to walk any further than I had to, the warm covers beckoning to me, waiting and ready to envelop me in plushness. As I placed my hands on the bed, my knee following me as I clumsily climbed on top, something stopped me.

It was hard.

It groaned as my knee came down on a very sensitive area.

It was a man.

Scrambling for my footing, shock and terror ripped through me as I stumbled backward and fell flat on my ass. *Thud!* My head caught the edge of the wall, instantly bringing tears to my eyes.

So much for my headache going away.

As the pain invaded, I clutched the back of my skull, cursing out loud as if I was by myself.

But I wasn't by myself.

Someone was in my room with me.

In my bed.

"Jesus Christ!" a gruff voice exclaimed. "Are you all right?" Before I could answer, the light flicked on, blinding me instantly. It took me a good minute to be able to adjust to the blaring intrusion, my eyes opening and closing so often I looked like I had some sort of nervous twitch.

The mystery man, a guy I'd not even looked at yet, reached down and gripped my arms. He pulled me to my feet and held me steady as I collected myself. Once my eyes adjusted, I shrugged off his hold and took a step back.

I should have been more afraid than I was. I should have been screaming and running for my life. But I wasn't. There was something about his presence which calmed me, as weird as it sounded. Still trying my best to be cautious, I took another step away from him and finally made eye contact, a smug smile on his face as my mouth dropped open in shock.

What the hell is he doing here? In my bed nonetheless?

"What are you doing here?" I asked as my eyes slowly scanned him from head to toe. I felt his warmth enclose me when he helped me to my feet. What I didn't realize was the heat radiated off his naked body. Well, he had on black boxer briefs, but otherwise...he was naked.

The fine lines of his torso called to me. I wanted nothing more than to run my fingertips over his hard form, imagining gripping his broad shoulders as he pinned me to the wall behind me. His thighs were thick and muscular, his ass no doubt perfection, as well.

Plopping back down on the bed, he nestled in and crossed his arms over his chest. I had no doubt he was settling in for the long haul. My eyes were so busy studying him, I missed what he said. I heard a faint sound, but I couldn't make out the actual words. Once my eyes connected with his, I faltered. "What did you say?" I asked, still a little lightheaded from smacking my head.

"You asked me what I was doing here, and I answered you." The corners of his lips turned up, revealing a perfect, white set of teeth. His dark hair was a tad unruly but in a run-my-hands-through-it type of way. Stubble was already starting to form on his jawline, his need to shave every day was most likely quite a hassle.

"And what was your answer?" I almost missed what he said again. It wasn't my fault, though. I was only human, after all.

A full-on laugh escaped him as he kept his eyes on me. "I said, you were very drunk last night and I needed to make sure you got home okay." A few more minutes passed before either one of us spoke. I was still in some sort of daze, wondering not only what the hell happened but how he came to bring me home. *And why did he stay?* "Sara, are you okay? Is it your head?" he asked, looking on with concern. I remained silent, for longer than was comfortable.

When still I didn't utter a word, he broke the ever-growing tension. Sort of. "Why are you staring at me like that, woman?" he grunted. "You're making me think things. Bad things." *Is he teasing me? Or tormenting me?*

"I'm not staring at you," I lied. Bringing my fingers to my forehead, I started to rub. "I just don't understand. What happened last night?" Admittedly, I was rather embarrassed I'd let things get out of hand, not remembering a goddamn thing. I made a promise to myself a long time ago to never let anything interfere with my well-being, to always be aware of my surroundings. *I guess I really messed up.*

As I moved around the other side of the bed, I realized my state of undress, with only a white T-shirt and cotton panties covering the most intimate of places. Diving under the comforter to cover up, embarrassment stole over my skin, something which he found amusing.

My awkwardness quickly disappeared, irritation taking its place. "Are you ever going to tell me what happened, or are you going to just sit there and laugh at me?" I quipped, the tone in my voice a little more than harsh.

"Sorry," he mumbled before he began the tale of the previous evening. "Considering how drunk you were, I'm not surprised you don't remember anything. Although," he continued as he put his hand over his heart, "I'm a little upset you don't remember what happened between us."

Taking a deep breath and preparing for the worst, I slowly opened my mouth to speak. "What do you mean?" I crouched further down the bed, regret slowly weaving its way through me. "Please don't tell me we had sex."

"Why, would that be so awful if we did?" he asked, looking offended.

The thing about being in a surprising situation was sometimes your mouth didn't filter what your brain was thinking. My response was one such example. "Yes, it would. I'd like to remember my first time." I brought the blanket up to cover my mouth as if the simple gesture would erase what I'd just said.

Yes, I was a twenty-six year old virgin. While some would consider my age too old to still be inexperienced, there was a good reason I chose to stay away from men.

A past which killed my trust in people.

When I heard him suck in a breath of air, I turned toward him, my eyes lingering a little too long on his mouth. "*That's* what you're comment meant," he said, the look on his face priceless, as if he'd just discovered the meaning of life.

"What comment?" *Oh, God, what the hell did I say?*

"Last night. When we were in the hallway, you told me you wanted me to be your first. I thought you were talking about a one-night stand." He rolled onto his side and leaned in closer. "I have to admit, while the thought of you picking me for your first one-nighter, or so I thought that's what you meant, was flattering, it was also upsetting." When I knitted my brow in confusion, he explained. "Going home with some random stranger is very dangerous, Sara. You really need to be more careful. Actually, scratch that. You don't have to worry about ever doing that again."

"Why?" *Oh, now I'm really curious.*

"Because."

"Because why?"

Air escaped his tempting mouth, his frustration beyond obvious. "Because I'll keep a better eye on you. Make sure you never drink that much again. That's why."

Satisfied he'd had his say, he rolled onto his back, staring straight ahead as if he was carefully choosing his next words.

My pulse quickened. My heart picked up pace, ramming hard against my chest. I literally felt my face become red in anger. *Who does this guy think he is trying to dictate what I do or don't do from now on?*

Never mind he was completely right. My actions the night before *were* careless. I knew it. But I'd never admit that to him.

"What makes you think you have any say over what I do?" I scoffed. "I'm a grown woman who can make her own decisions. Good or bad."

"Not if I have anything to say about it," he retorted. "Never again, Sara. I mean it."

It was then I realized he'd said my name a few times and I didn't even know his. Or at least I didn't think I did.

Before I could think of a comment to his ludicrous statement, he jumped out of bed and started getting dressed, pulling on his jeans first before throwing his shirt over his head. Sitting back down on the edge of the mattress, he leaned down and reached for his shoes. After he'd finished, he stood to his full height and locked eyes on me once again.

"Are you leaving?" I asked, sounding a little desperate. I didn't even wait for him to answer before I fired off another question. "I thought you were going to tell me what happened last night."

"Oh, yeah," he smugly said. Without missing a beat, he dove right in. "What do you remember? Anything at all?"

"I remember going out with my friends and having a few drinks, but other than that...no." I turned my head, embarrassed I couldn't recall any other details.

"Well, I saw you there. At Throttle. I helped you carry drinks back to your table before you casually dismissed me." *There's that offended look again.* A few moments of silence passed before he continued to speak. "Anyway, I saw you again on your way back from the bathroom and then we..." he trailed off.

"We what?"

"We had a little moment in the hallway." *That's it? That's all he's giving me?* I wanted to scream but I kept my temper in check.

"Seriously? You aren't going to tell me what happened?" I asked, crossing my arms over my chest.

"We had a moment," he repeated before he made his way toward the door. "Oh, and by the way...I'm Alek Devera," he offered.

I guess I hadn't known his name after all.

As he pulled the door open, he briefly turned toward me, a weird expression appearing out of nowhere. Trying to decipher the look on his gorgeous face was too much so early in the morning.

So I just gave up.

It didn't matter, though.

I'd never see him again anyway.

Or so I thought.

~1~

Sara

One Week Earlier

My day had started off well. I actually got up when my alarm went off. I was having a good hair day. My mood was anticipatory. *Let's just hope everything plays out the way I need it to.*

I had a meeting with my bank to discuss a small business loan, my proposal all ready for them to review. Desperate for my life to start heading on the path to something good, I wished and prayed this appointment would turn in my favor.

I was ready to head out the door then realized I couldn't find my damn keys.

"Alexa!" I yelled, running around like a crazy woman.

"What the hell are you hollering for so early in the morning?" Alexa was like me in that she loved to sleep in until noon if the desire struck her. So for her, ten in the morning on a Saturday was still too early.

"Sorry, but I'm going to be late for my appointment and I can't find my keys."

"They're on the kitchen table, you loon. I can see them from here," she remarked as she leaned against her bedroom doorframe.

"Thanks, girl. I owe you one."

"You can pick up some lunch on your way home. I'd like some Chinese food, please. You know what I like." Once she barked out her order, she closed her door and most likely went back to sleep. I didn't have the heart to tell her I was going to the shop right after the bank. *Oh, well, I'll just text her later.*

~ ~ ~ ~

A little over a year before, I'd moved to Seattle with my best friend, Alexa. I'd lucked out and landed a job at a cute little florist shop close to our apartment. I was thankful for the short commute because, out of the two of us, Alexa was the one who owned a car. She'd let me borrow it whenever necessary but otherwise, I walked wherever else I needed to go.

Every day that passed, I was eternally grateful to have her in my life. Alexa Bearnheart was the kind of person you definitely wanted in your corner. Two years my senior, we'd bonded quickly in high school.

When I'd told her I wanted to get a fresh start and move somewhere I wasn't constantly reminded of my past, she followed me, packing her bags and never looking back.

"How did it go at the bank, honey?" Lost in thought of my dear friend, I hadn't seen Katherine approach as I walked through the front door of the shop. I'd become rather close to the old woman over the past year, her nurturing ways something I'd most definitely needed during the huge transition in my life.

She was a stout woman with a friendly face, her hair short and mostly white. She hadn't bothered coloring it since she said she greyed way too fast the more the years ticked by. "A waste of money," she would say.

"I think it went very well. Mr. Hemsworth took my proposal and said they would let me know for sure in a week if I was approved to take over this gem of a place." I smiled, hoping I didn't run into any complications. Katherine had told me she was ready to retire, offering me the chance to buy Full Bloom.

"I'm sure everything will work out for you, honey. For both of us."

I really hoped so. I was in desperate need for a normal life after everything I'd been through.

I loved working for Katherine, but nothing would compare to actually owning the place. She had an excellent customer base, having been in business for over forty years. We'd seen it all, from women coming in to buy an arrangement for a special occasion to the men who'd messed up with their significant other, some coming in almost monthly to try and smooth things over.

Hello! Stop messing up!

Then again, that would hurt business, so...

Since I actually had to work, I walked toward the counter and placed my purse underneath, preparing for a hectic Saturday. Grabbing a stack of invoices, I settled in and got busy.

Normally, I'd pitch in and help make deliveries whenever we were shorthanded but both Matt and Pete were there. We also had a few part-timers coming in later to assist, as well.

Pete was Katherine's cousin. He loved helping her out when he could, but he was also considering retiring.

Being the nice guy he was, he said he'd wait until the sale was final, giving me enough time to try and find someone else.

Matt was closer to my age and had been working for Katherine for about four years. He told me he adored flowers and loved working with them. Whenever he wasn't in the best of moods, they would work their magic and lift his gloomy spirits.

We'd actually gone out a few times to eat, catch a movie or grab the occasional drink. Sometimes, Alexa would even come with us, hanging out until the early morning hours.

Initially, I had a small crush on Matt when I'd first met him. Who wouldn't? He was quite the looker. At six-feet tall, he towered over my five-foot six-inch frame. He wasn't gigantic by any means, but I did have to look up when I was standing next to him, especially without any heels on. Naturally wavy, dark blond hair adorned the top of his head, styled to perfection each and every time. His physique resembled one of a male model; he even had the wardrobe to boot. His eyes were a brilliant blue color, and he had one of the most genuine, endearing smiles I'd ever seen.

I was aware of the reaction he obtained from women when we went out together, but he never paid any attention to it. Sometimes, I thought I caught him sneaking a peek at other guys. Deep down, I knew he was attracted to men, but I never brought it up. If he wanted to tell me, then he would, in his own time. Needless to say, our relationship had never been anything more than a platonic friendship, which I was completely happy with, especially considering my little crush had dissolved and was replaced with genuine friendship.

I was in the front of the shop working on the computer, when Katherine's voice startled me.

"Thank goodness you're good with that computer, honey," she said over my shoulder as she passed by with a huge display of beautiful white and pink lilies. Even though the particular display was more on the simple side, she really was an artist in her own right. A customer could point to a variety of different flowers and she would somehow know the right way to arrange them. What to put where, plucking out anything which didn't belong. Every single arrangement she made was a pure masterpiece, which was probably why she did very well for herself.

I just hoped I could do my part to continue the legacy she'd spent forty-six years building.

Lost in thought, I nearly jumped out of my skin when the phone rang.

"Hello, thank you for calling Full Bloom. How may I help you today?" I went on autopilot taking all of the information for the order, from the date and time of delivery to the type of arrangement needed.

"Do you want the card to say anything in particular?" I asked the man on the other end of phone. "Okay, let me read that back to you. 'Sorry for missing our anniversary last week. I love you. Tom.'"

I shook my head and grinned. *Typical.* But it was good for business, so I couldn't complain.

Once the order was complete, I put it in the pile for the following day's deliveries, first giving Katherine a heads-up I needed a mixed dozen of red and white roses. Thankfully, it wasn't for that day, because I didn't think we would be able to accommodate on such short notice. Roses were a very popular go-to flower for a lot of people, and I thought I'd seen the last of them in the back room being wrapped up for one of the current orders.

For the next couple hours, I answered the phone, entered invoices and double-checked Katherine had all of the order slips so she could make sure she had the flowers to make up each and every presentation.

We didn't typically get a ton of walk-ins. I deduced people preferred to look up our website, pick out what they wanted, and simply call it in. But I guessed it *was* the digital age, after all. One could simply give you their credit card information over the phone and get on with life.

I found it odd sometimes most people didn't even want to write out their own cards, especially the really personal ones. Some of them were quite deplorable. One time, I had a guy tell me he wanted me to write, 'Sorry I slept with your sister'. I actually made him repeat himself to ensure I'd heard him right. Suffice it to say, he didn't spend any unnecessary time on the phone with me.

I was in the middle of pounding away on the keyboard when I heard the bell above the door. Knowing most customers browsed the ready-made displays, I kept my head down and continued working.

All of a sudden, I felt a presence across the counter from me, instantly making me feel strange.

Then I heard his voice. Deep and gravelly. "Excuse me, Miss. Can you help me?" he serenely asked.

The hairs on the back of my neck stood up, goose bumps breaking out all over my body.

All of this and I still hadn't even looked up yet.

Slowly raising my head, I prepared myself as best I could to see who was causing me to have such a reaction. When my eyes finally landed on his face, I actually felt myself wobble a bit, grabbing onto the edge of the counter to steady myself.

What the hell is happening to me?

He was the most stunning male specimen I'd ever had the pleasure of feasting my eyes on. He was almost too much; like looking directly at the sun. Fearing he was going to think I was rude or just plain weird, I tried not to stare for too long. Too bad my brain wasn't communicating with my trembling body.

He had the most perfectly sculpted face, almost as if the gods used him as a blank canvas, gifting him the best attributes imaginable. But the one feature which really garnered my attention was his eyes. The most beautiful shade of dark green I'd ever seen. They seemed to hold the power to captivate with just one glance.

His hair was a very dark, 'chocolate brown yet almost black' shade of color. The freshly tousled style was a tad longer all around than I was typically attracted to. But it worked. On him.

He was wearing what looked to be a very expensive dark grey suit, the red tie giving it a small pop of color. I could tell he had broad shoulders, but because the suit covered everything else, I had to use my imagination as to what was underneath.

The guy looked like he had money and didn't make any apologies for it. But he also appeared as someone who wasn't conceited or purposefully showy; just knew what he had. *How can I tell all this by simply looking at him?* I guessed it was just a strong feeling.

I spoke only when I regained some of my composure, which in reality was only a few seconds from when I first saw him. "What can I do to you? Uh, for you? What can I do *for* you?"

That's it, Sara. Emphasize the for *you.*

His reaction was one of amusement. "I'd like to purchase some flowers and have them delivered tomorrow. At one o'clock precisely."

"Did you mess up with your wife or girlfriend?" I asked before I could stop myself.

What is wrong with me?

He smirked, cocked his head and explained, "They're for a friend. She recently had surgery, and I thought it would be a nice gesture to help cheer her up."

"Isn't that a little misleading?" *Seriously, what is wrong with me?*

Why was I being so blunt and forward with him? Probably because I couldn't filter what I was thinking before it flew out of my stupid mouth.

He laughed and asked, "How so?"

"Never mind. I don't know why I asked you that. It's none of my business. I'm sorry." I was sure my face was three shades of red, my embarrassment taking a fierce hold.

"Don't apologize. It's nice to have a conversation with someone when they actually say what they mean." Taking a step back, his gaze never left my face. It must have been a good minute before he spoke again. "I have to tell you...I find you a bit intriguing."

Me? Intriguing? I didn't know about that, but I was sure my bluntness was a rarity for him. Something told me people yes'd him to death, telling him only what they thought he wanted to hear.

"Hey, Sara, did you see the order slip for the Canter Road delivery today? I've looked everywhere and can't find it."

Matt came around the corner, looking like a madman searching for lost treasure. He appeared panicked until I handed him the slip over my shoulder, winking at him in the process.

"You are a lifesaver, girl. What would I ever do without you?" He gave me his thousand-watt smile and headed back toward the prep room, but not before giving me a big smooch on the cheek.

Normally, I wouldn't have given his actions a second thought but considering I had an audience, I became a little flustered by the extra attention being thrown my way.

"Is he your boyfriend?" the gorgeous stranger asked, a blend of emotions evident in his tone. *Is that curiosity mixed with annoyance?* Now *he* was the one asking inappropriate questions. He was making me anxious, and I didn't even fully understand why.

Since he flustered me, I didn't know what to say except, "What?"

With a cocked eyebrow, he repeated more sternly, "Is he your boyfriend?" He leaned forward on the counter, his hands practically touching my own.

Whoa. Who did this guy think he was? His tone floored me. His face was the picture of composure, throwing me off because the two didn't match up.

I wasn't going to answer him. I really wasn't, but something clicked inside me. The need to assure him Matt and I were not an item was simply too strong.

"No, Matt is just a very good friend of mine."

"Uh-huh," was all he mumbled, his bottom lip disappearing between his teeth. Normally, I would have rushed to get this cocky man out of the store, but I couldn't force myself to want to part with his domineering presence.

After composing myself yet again, I attempted to continue with my normal line of questioning, making sure this time they were of the appropriate nature. "What kind of flowers would you like to send to this friend of yours?" *I couldn't help myself.* "And what's the address where they're being delivered?"

"Why don't you surprise me and put together something of your liking?"

Is he serious? Why would he want me to put together something out of the blue, without any input from him whatsoever? "I don't know if that is such a good idea. I mean, I have no inkling as to what kind of flowers she likes, what color she prefers or anything like that."

"I'm sure whatever you come up with will be perfect. I trust you." He wrote down the delivery address, placed a wad of bills on the counter and turned around, walking out the door before I could even respond.

~2~

Sara

The rest of the week went by in a flash due to how busy we always were. Closed on Sundays, I always tried to take full advantage of Saturday nights. It was my one night to hang out and let loose with two of my favorite people, Matt and Alexa.

"Matt, what are your plans tonight?" I was hoping he was game for hanging out, especially since I needed to stop reminiscing over my encounter with Mr. Gorgeous from almost a week ago.

"I'm free. Whatcha thinking?" he asked, cleaning up the remaining orders scattered on the counter.

"I'd like to hit up that new nightclub, Throttle. Have you ever been there? I hear decent things, and now is as good a time as any to check it out. What do you say?" *Please say yes, please say yes.*

"Sounds all right to me. Is Alexa going? And what time do you want me to pick you up?" Initially, I'd thought Matt was interested in Alexa, but that idea was quickly squashed once I realized he might only like the romantic company of men.

"I already texted her and she's in. But you don't have to pick us up. We can just meet you there at nine o'clock. You know it's gonna take us girls a while to get ready," I teased. I felt bad because every time he swung by to pick us up, he always ended up waiting at least forty-five minutes for us to finish primping ourselves.

"I'm going to finish up with this last order and head on home. I'll see you guys later tonight then!" he yelled over his shoulder as he headed toward the back of the store.

An hour later, I'd made my way outside and inhaled the fresh air. It smelled like rain but then again, it frequently smelled like that. This *was* Seattle, after all. But I wasn't going to let some precipitation put a damper on what was surely going to be a great night out with friends.

It was almost six-thirty when I finally arrived home. Unlocking the front door, I breathed a sigh of relief when I entered my solace.

I really felt comfortable in the apartment I shared with Alexa, even though our space was a bit on the small side. But it was ours and it was homey. It took us a while to find the right décor; thankfully, we had the same taste. I wasn't sure what the name was for our style. Was it contemporary or modern? Or maybe it was something different altogether.

Rich browns, creams and reds decorated our small living room. Only a few pieces of furniture adorned the space, the comfy leather recliner the object of many a bet as to who was going to enjoy it on any given night.

Our kitchen was also small but it had come with up-to-date appliances, a cost-saving benefit to the both of us. The kitchen island gave way to four stools which slid underneath. More savings.

For as small as the living room and kitchen were, we lucked out with the size of the bedrooms and the one bathroom we shared. The much larger spaces allowed us to fit all of our other furniture and belongings.

Like I said, we were very lucky to find the place. It wasn't cheap, but it wasn't as pricey as some of the other places we'd looked at. Splitting the bills right down the middle left us both with a little extra cash to splurge on whatever else we liked. One of those splurges was going to be the night's fun at Throttle.

"Hey, Sara!" Alexa shouted. "I didn't even hear you come in. Can you come back here? I need your fashion opinion." Alexa had more clothes than I think she knew what to do with, piles of outfits strewn all over her room. I honestly didn't know how she ever found anything.

She was holding up a short, navy blue dress as I walked into her room. Other options were laid out on top of her bed, in case that one didn't pan out.

"It's nice, but isn't it a bit short? Aren't you worried you'll be showing off your goodies?"

"If I'm lucky, yes!" she exclaimed, a big grin on her beautiful face. I knew Lex was not easy or slutty or anything like that. But you really couldn't tell by the way she dressed sometimes. I personally wasn't comfortable dressing like she did, something she was forever trying to change.

"If you like it, then I'm sure you'll look great." There was no use in defending my position because she was going to wear what she wanted. Sometimes I didn't even know why she asked my opinion.

"What are you going to wear tonight? And please don't say jeans and a T-shirt." *All right, so she knew me a little too well.*

"Well...yeah. I don't have anything else." I really did need to go shopping for some new clothes. What I had was nice, but I didn't have *club* clothes. But a piece here and there couldn't really hurt, as long as it was to my taste, and length.

"Here, I have the perfect dress for you." She went into that packed closet of hers and almost fell over something trying to reach to the left to pull an item out.

It was a beautiful, hunter-green dress, with a plunging neckline the main focus. The back of it was no more modest, a large opening scooping down to pretty much show off the top of my ass. As if that wasn't enough, the length barely covered my lady parts.

"You're kidding, right? I would never wear that out in public. First of all, it's way too short. I'm a good three inches taller than you, so it would be *that* much shorter on me. And second of all, I couldn't possibly wear a bra because of how open the back is."

"So then don't wear a bra."

"Are you out of your mind? Do you know what I would look like with no bra?" I was too well endowed to never wear support. I wasn't gargantuan, but I had too much to ever go without a bra, in public at least.

"You have a great rack, Sara. You don't take enough advantage of your *gifts*." She was already laughing because she knew I found it funny when she referred to my breasts as *gifts*. I shook my head and smiled.

"I'm not wearing that dress, so if you don't have anything else, I'm going to find my jeans and T-shirt." I turned on my heel and left her standing there with her mouth open.

"Wait, I think I have something else that'll meet your approval." I heard her rummaging around in her room again before she came barging into my space, quickly shoving something into my hands. It was a red sparkly tank-top accompanied by a white skirt. Another short item, although the skirt wasn't as short as her other clothing.

"Why haven't I ever seen you wear this before?" I asked as I pointed to the piece of clothing. "Is it new?"

"No, it's just too long on me." *Figures.* "Will you at least try it on? See how great you look?"

"All right, I'll try it on only to shut you up," I said, throwing her another smile over my shoulder.

"I'll be right back," she retorted. "I think I have the perfect shoes to go with it, should you grace me with your approval of wearing it."

I checked the size before I did anything. Even though we were different heights, we sometimes fit into the same size pants and skirts. Not that I wore a lot of her clothes, for obvious reasons. The top was bigger than she usually bought so I was wondering if she didn't buy this for me, secretly hoping to push me out of my more conservative wear. I wouldn't put it past her. "Why did you buy the wrong size shirt?" I asked as she came back into my room.

"I grabbed it by accident and didn't feel like taking it back to the store." *Uh-huh.*

After I'd quickly thrown on the clothes, I stood in front of the mirror and smoothed everything out. Surprisingly, everything fit the way I'd want it to. The skirt hit me mid-thigh, a length I could definitely work with. The top, while tight to my chest, looked amazing.

"What do you think?" I asked as I twirled around in front of her.

"Holy fuck, girl! You look so hot! You have to know how good you look right now, Sara." She was hopeful I would agree with her.

"To be honest, I think I do look nice, but I don't know about this," I said as I waved my hand back and forth over the top of the shirt, pointing to the obvious. "Don't you think it looks a little sleazy?"

"Not at all. I think you look fantastic. Here's the shoes." She handed me a pair of nude wedges. Thankfully we wore the same size. I had to admit with the shoes, I really did like the outfit. It accentuated all of my curves and made me look...sexy.

"You were right. I look good, although I'm still not a hundred percent sold on the shirt. But I'll work with it. Thanks, Lex."

"I knew you would come over to my side one day."

"Just for tonight," I chuckled.

It was already 7:15, which meant I only had a little over an hour to get ready. We had to allot at least twenty minutes to drive to the club.

I dried my long chestnut-colored hair as quickly as possible, running a big curling iron through it to smooth it out and give me some nice bouncy, loose curls. I wore minimal makeup, some sheer eyeshadow, a little eyeliner and mascara, some blush and a clear lip gloss. I thought the outfit was enough already; I didn't want to add to the dramatics with an overdone face.

I was officially done with fifteen minutes to spare, so I sauntered into Alexa's room to see how she was coming along. She was almost ready as well, putting the finishing touches on her own makeup. She really did look beautiful, even with the revealing clothing she chose. She had shoulder-length, dark blonde hair with sun-kissed highlights. It was her natural color, and almost everyone complimented her on it. Her pale blue eyes and olive complexion were a great contrast to her tresses. Alexa really was quite the looker, and I made sure to tell her as much.

"You look really beautiful tonight, Lex. You're going to have to fight the men off for sure."

"You look fantastic, too. We're going to have a great time." She laughed as she did a little dance. "Thankfully Matt will be there to get rid of anyone we don't want bothering us." Sometimes we had Matt act as a boyfriend, warding off guys who couldn't take the hint.

One more quick glance in the mirror and we were off to enjoy our evening.

~3~

Sara

By the time we found a parking spot and walked to the front of the club, it was just after nine o'clock. Matt was waiting for us on the sidewalk, looking like he'd stepped right out of a J Crew ad. Wearing dark jeans, a fitted light grey polo shirt and brown boots, he was quite the sight to behold. He was one of the few guys I saw who could look good with wearing his collar up.

After we finished greeting one another, we glanced at the line and realized it snaked around the corner. I really wanted to go in, but I wasn't too sure about the long-ass wait.

"Come on, guys, let's go," Matt said as he grabbed each of our hands and pulled us toward the guy with the clipboard.

"Matt, don't we have to go to the end of the line?" I asked, eyeing up the other waiting customers.

"No, I know one of the bartenders working tonight. He said he would put us on the list. So let's go, shall we?" I instantly reached up and kissed him on his gorgeous cheek, thankful he had connections.

As soon as we walked in, we noticed how big the place was, much larger than it looked from the outside. Private sitting areas littered either side of the enormous room, each with four black leather sofas running the length of each wall.

It was cozy while still managing to be classy.

The dance floor was smack-dab in the middle of the space, the house music at a tolerable level. People were already busy having a great time, swaying and grinding to the beats thrumming through the large speaker system.

There was a very large bar straight ahead and an area set up for actual bands to play. There wasn't anyone scheduled that night, though, which was a little disappointing. I loved to discover new music. Local talent was certainly in abundance around our area.

As we walked, we almost missed the second floor towering above us, a DJ booth hidden in the center of it. So that's *where the music is coming from.*

First impressions were everything, and Throttle was a club I could definitely see us coming to over and over again.

"Let's head back to the bar to grab some drinks before it becomes way too crowded for us to even order anything," Alexa hollered over the increasing music.

"Don't worry about it. My friend Colin said he's working the bar. I just have to find him." Matt grabbed both of our hands again and led us toward our drink hookup.

Finding him easily enough, we had our double orders in less than five minutes. I tried not to make eye contact with the people who had obviously been waiting before us. I could feel them giving us the evil eye.

We were lucky enough to find an open seating area, enough room for all three of us. "I can definitely see us coming here a lot," Alexa voiced as she winked at some random guy passing by with his friends. She didn't waste any time. I wasn't as aggressive, which was totally okay with me. But I couldn't fault her for her forwardness, either. She knew what she wanted and she went for it.

I was envious of that kind of confidence.

"Lex, can we be here for twenty minutes before you start stalking your prey?" Matt asked as he hit her shoulder with his, giving her a wink.

She laughed. "You know me better than that by now, sweetie."

"I do." He looked over at me and shrugged, knowing Alexa would continue to be Alexa, no matter what.

We'd been sitting for about an hour before we needed a refill. Since Matt bought us the first round, I announced I would go for the next one. I wasn't sure whether or not Colin would remember me from a two-second introduction an hour before, but I would give it a shot.

I made my way through the ever-growing crowd, knocking into a few people on my way. *How am I going to make it back without spilling everything all over myself, or someone else for that matter?*

I was able to spot him right away, and thankfully he remembered I was Matt's friend. "More of the same for all of you?" I couldn't believe he remembered what we were all drinking, but I guess it was his job. It was still impressive nonetheless.

Trying my best to figure out how I was going to carry six drinks back to our area, I was startled when I felt warm breath on my skin.

Then I heard a voice.

"Do you need help with those?"

The hairs on the back of my neck instantly prickled.

That voice!

It couldn't be.

Sure enough, when I turned around I hit against his towering form, spilling part of a drink all over his shoe.

It was Mr. Sexy from earlier in the week. *What the hell is he doing here? And how did he see me in this crowd?* I was lucky if I could even see my own friends, and I knew where they were sitting.

Stepping back, I was able to get a better look at him. And oh, was he quite the sight. His black shirt fit him like a glove, a hint of an exquisite body underneath. He cuffed the material up to his elbows, exposing his sexy forearms. Dark-washed jeans hung seductively on his hips, teasing and tormenting the hell out of me.

He looked......opulent.

His hair was behaving in that unruly way, looking as if he was constantly running his hands through it. Sexy was what it was. I longed to run my fingers through it, twisting his soft strands around my hand as I pulled him into me.

Holy Christ. Get a hold of yourself, woman!

Being in close proximity to him was a dangerous game. His intoxicating male scent surrounded me, automatically making me even more aroused than I was a second ago.

His pheromones were sending mine into overdrive.

He was enchanting.

I have to get away from him.

"Did you need some help?" he asked again, patiently waiting for my answer. Roving his eyes slowly over my face, he lingered on my lips before dipping lower to gaze at my displayed breasts. *This damn shirt.*

His look descended my body until he reached my feet, then ever so slowly raised them back up to meet my eyes. Eventually. I felt so vulnerable, as if I was standing naked in front of him. Parting his mouth, he slowly ran this tongue over his bottom lip, a lip I suddenly wanted to bite. Without realizing it, I mimicked his actions, running my tongue slowly over the sensitive skin.

Quickly regaining my wits, I finally answered him.

"No, thanks. I can manage just fine by myself." I was trying to pretend like I didn't remember him, trying not to appear affected by his mere presence. I didn't think I was too convincing though.

"I insist." Before I could protest, he grabbed four of the six drinks, turned and waited for me to follow him. He was obviously not taking no for an answer.

"Fine," was the only thing I could think to respond. He was making me uneasy again but in a purely sexual way. My breathing had changed, inhaling and expelling quick, shallow breaths. My nipples had become painfully erect, pushing against the thin fabric of my shirt. It was definitely not cold in the club, so I knew it was my reaction to him standing so close to me. A deep ache started to bloom between my thighs, making me hyperaware my body was betraying the distant persona I was trying to give off. Never before had any man affected me so deeply.

He led the way to where we were sitting, which was a surprise since

I barely knew my own way back. But I followed him, and sure enough he stopped right in front of both of my friends. They glanced first at him then over to me with questioning eyes.

"Who's your friend?" Alexa immediately asked. I could see her delight as she was taking him all in, top to bottom, stopping longer than necessary when her eyes hit his *package*. When she finally ripped her eyes away, her mouth agape and practically drooling, she connected her gaze with mine. I laughed. Her blatant perusal of Mr. Sexy was too funny, and I couldn't help myself. Thankfully he was oblivious, or at least I thought he was.

"I don't know, and he's not staying." I didn't mean to come off as rude as I sounded, but I couldn't stand the fact a stranger was making me feel that way, pitting my body against my brain. I grabbed the rest of the drinks from his hand and put them down on the table. When I finally happened to look over at Matt, I noticed he was glaring at our visitor. I instantly shifted my gaze and saw Mr. Sexy returning Matt's glower.

Both men looked pissed, for reasons unknown to me. But I knew enough about testosterone to realize I should put some distance between them both. Although Matt was in excellent shape, this guy had a good couple inches on him, not to mention a few more pounds of muscle. Plus, I didn't want to put Matt in the position to defend me, like he did sometimes. He had become somewhat protective over me when we were out together. Maybe it was because I was kind of on the shyer side when it came to dealing with people I didn't really know. I stuck up for myself when necessary, but I didn't like confrontation unless it was unavoidable.

I turned around toward the relative stranger and instinctively put my hand on his arm, pushing him away from our table. *Shit! His arm is even more rock-solid than it looks.* Yeah, I had to remove him before Matt said something. "You can go now. Thanks for your help," I mumbled, still trying to rein in my overactive hormones. When I turned back around, I could still feel him standing behind me for a brief moment.

"I'll see you real soon," he said, his voice like velvet coating my ears.

Shivers instantly wracked my body.

Then he was gone.

~4~

Sara

"Wasn't that the guy from earlier this week? How did he know you would be here? Do you know him?" Matt was shooting off questions at me quicker than I could even think of the answers.

"Yes, it is and no, I don't know him. I don't know what he's doing here. He saw me at the bar and offered to help me bring the drinks back over." That was a true account of what happened, leaving out the part of how my body reacted to him. Even after he was gone.

"There's something about him I don't trust. Be careful if you meet up with him again, Sara." Matt was concerned for me; I could see it written all over his face. *But it's not like I keep running into the man. He knows where I work and now he has seen me at the club. Does that mean I should stay away from this place now?* I knew it was my first time there, but I was kind of planning on coming quite often in the future, especially since Matt had someone on the inside who could give us some VIP treatment, so to speak.

"You never mentioned anything about a God-like creature coming into the shop this week. Seriously, Sara, how could you forget to mention *that* man?" Alexa was still trying to scope out the crowd to see if she could catch another glimpse of him. She was so obvious.

What I couldn't understand was why her interest in him was suddenly bothering me. I hardly knew him, yet I had an unexplainable jealousy emanating from not that deep down. I'd never had this feeling about anyone before, especially someone I'd just met. I secretly mocked women who were jealous of others around their men; too much emotional energy.

Or so I always thought.

"I didn't mention it because he's not worth mentioning. I don't know him. He came into the shop to buy flowers for a *friend*," I said, using air quotes, "who had surgery recently, and he thought it would be a nice gesture. I told him it was misleading to her but...whatever."

They both stared at me with a puzzled look in their eyes. "Who are you trying to kid, girly girl? You like him; otherwise, why the hell would you remember your conversation with him? You can't fool us, Sara." Alexa laughed. "Plus, you're a terrible liar." I fumbled with a comeback to her absurd observation, but I had nothing.

I couldn't really think of anything to say which would convince them—or maybe myself—I wasn't interested so I simply responded with, "I don't know what to tell you. Can we please talk about something else?"

Since Alexa knew she wasn't getting any more out of me about him,
she decided to move on to other topics. Shopping, food and men were
at the top of her list, which I was completely fine with.

After about another hour or so, we were all due for another refill or
two. It was Alexa's turn to secure our drinks, so Matt and I sat back
and got comfortable. She gave a little pout but headed off toward the
bar. It was nearing 11:30 and the place was pretty much at full
capacity.

Alexa was back in no time thankfully, due to Colin still working the
bar and not being on break. As soon as she took her seat, I decided to
make my way to the ladies room, if I could only find it first. She said
she saw one to the left of the bar, underneath the stairwell.

"I'll be right back, guys. Watch my drink." I hastily made my way
through the throngs of people and ended up behind six women waiting
in line for the same purpose. Needless to say, after a few drinks, I
really had to use the facilities and the longer I waited, the more I
realized it. Thankfully, everyone was relatively quick so I was in and
out in less than ten minutes.

Just as I was rounding the corner, someone grabbed my hand and
pulled me into a dark section of the hallway. I instantly panicked,
having flashbacks, until I smelled *him*. His scent was positively
intoxicating, and I was instantly put at ease.

Emotionally, not sexually.

As with our last close encounter, a dull ache between my legs, made me slip deeper and deeper into some sort of daze. His hand was still covering mine, and I grew warmer by the second.

"I'm glad I had the chance to run into you again before I left," he mumbled as he stepped closer.

"How did you know where I was? Did you follow me to the ladies room?" Why was I secretly hoping he would say yes?

"Not at all. I saw you walk by and reacted. Hope you don't mind?" His smugness was almost off-putting.

Almost.

I yanked my hand from his warm grip and said the first thought which came to mind.

"I really don't have anything to talk to you about, so if you'll excuse me, I have to be getting back to my friends now."

He leaned down closer to my face, so close I thought he was going to kiss me. "I don't think you want to go anywhere. In fact, I think you want to stay right here. With me. Tell me I'm wrong."

"You're wrong," I said with mock defiance.

"Why are you lying?" His tone indicated he was a little irritated, but

I wasn't sure why exactly. "You can't deny there's an attraction between us. Why don't you just go with it and see what happens?" His warm breath fanned my face, tickling my mouth in the most delicious way. Leaning closer, he asked, "Can I kiss you?" His question certainly surprised me. I doubted he was a man who asked permission for anything and the fact he sought my consent told me he didn't want to overstep any boundaries.

It was sweet.

It was torture.

Resting my hands on his chest, my initial reaction was to push him away. *My God, his chest is as hard as steel. I can feel every muscle definition perfectly.*

But he was right; there was an undeniable attraction between us, something I couldn't explain.

So I gave in.

"Yes," I whispered, my hands gripping the material of his shirt and pulling him into me. The *S* hadn't left my mouth before he was on me, devouring my breath as if he needed it to survive.

His kiss undid me. It was everything I'd read about in romance novels. It was everything I'd seen in those mushy, lovey-dovey movies. It was real. And it was happening to me. The first time his tongue softly stroked mine, I almost came on the spot. He was perfectly skilled, and artisan mastering his craft of seduction.

I'd completely lost myself, holding onto him and praying our moment would last forever.

He broke our connection, a move which left me wanting him even more. "I've been craving this for so long," he whispered before he was instantly back to consuming me with his perfect mouth. His statement flitted through my mind but quickly disappeared the more he teased me.

He tasted slightly of scotch, and mixed with all his other scents, it was quite overwhelming, but in a good way. I slowly inched my hands toward the back of his head. Snaking my fingers into his hair, I gripped him closer to my mouth. He groaned at my small display of enrapture, letting me know how aroused he was. Pushing me against the wall, he covered my body with his, pressing his lower half into my own. I could feel him straining against his jeans, something which made me even more excited. I didn't know what got into me, but I reached down and ran my palm over his erection.

His body twitched.

"Don't start something you won't be able to finish, woman," he growled into my mouth.

"Whatever do you mean?" I batted my eyelashes at him, toying with him a bit. I was playing innocent—well, not completely playing. Although I knew I wasn't going to really do anything, I wasn't completely sure why I was going to such lengths to tease him.

Maybe I wanted to make sure he was just as affected by me as I was by him.

"If you tease me too much, I don't think I'll be able to control myself," he panted.

"Then maybe we should stop." *Please, don't listen to me.*

"Is that what you really want?" He intently searched my face, trying to read my reaction to him and the current position in which we found ourselves. What he discovered was my need for him. I wanted him to start kissing me again, and I said as much by leaning back into him, enticing him to continue.

That time, he was a little more audacious. While his beautiful mouth stole the distance between us, one hand gingerly caressed my neck, slowly slipping down near my throat, then onto the top of my nearly exposed breasts. "You really shouldn't wear things like this. Every man in here has been staring at you, and it's driving me insane." He was saying all of this as his hand was massaging my breast, pulling gently at the top of my shirt.

"I think you're exaggerating a bit by *every man*, and what do you care what I wear?"

"I don't like how exposed you are." He snapped his lips closed, clearly aware he was stepping over some invisible boundary.

"You don't?" I found it funny he 'didn't like how exposed I was,' yet he was pulling at my tank top, revealing even more of me. But then again, we were in a dark corner of a hallway where we were fortunate to remain alone, away from everyone else.

When his eyes connected with mine again, they took on a darker hue, his pupils dilating in arousal. "This is only for me. Tell me," he moaned, flicking his tongue along the side of my throat. "Tell me this is only for me." He was still groping my breast, his lips teasing my skin, his other hand circling around to my backside. Grabbing me firmly, he pushed himself closer, almost crushing me under his own body.

I loved it.

I wanted it to be just for him.

No one else.

Just him.

"Tell me," he demanded again, my silence torturing him.

"Yes," I whispered. "Yes, it is all for you."

"Only me?"

"Only you," I responded, my breath barely escaping my mouth.

It was obvious the alcohol coursing through my veins was catching up with me, causing me to throw caution to the wind and engage in risky behavior with the man standing before me. "What do you want to do to me?" I couldn't believe I was behaving that way with a virtual stranger, albeit the sexiest, most intriguing man I'd ever had the pleasure of laying my eyes on. But he was still a man I didn't really know.

His lips made their way toward the sensitive spot underneath my earlobe. When he spoke in his seductive low timbre, I thought I would combust right then and there. "If we were alone, I would rip your clothes off and feast on your body. I would lick and suck you everywhere, especially here." His hand instantly went to the heat between my thighs. I groaned and slumped forward. Thankfully, he was there to make sure I wouldn't fall over. "Is that what you want? Is that what you would like me to do to you?"

Wow!

I couldn't concentrate on what he was asking me because his hand danced over my core, rubbing me in ways which should have been illegal. "Don't stop," I pleaded, snagging his lower lip and returning my own brand of sweet agony.

"You're going to undo me," he proclaimed. His words were confusing, their meaning completely lost on me. But I didn't care. All I wanted was for him to devour me, to crush my soul with his passion and need.

After a few minutes, he pulled away, air imminent for the both of us. "Do you even realize how fucked I am because of you?" What an odd question; although it did spark intrigue.

Before I could answer, he withdrew from me completely. His lips left mine wanting more of his taste. His fingers had offered a trail of heat my body was instantly missing. The look in his eyes even changed, reverting back to a man seemingly unaffected.

I couldn't help but wonder if I had done or said something wrong. Trying to think back over the past few minutes did nothing but prove frustrating. Entirely caught up in the way he made me feel left no room for reason. Failing to even comprehend what it could've been I'd said or done, his new demeanor was entirely lost on me.

So I gave up.

Not wanting our tryst to end, I started dreaming up ways to remain in his presence, something which was so unlike me. *I would love for you to be my first*, I thought.

"First what? What are you talking about?" he asked as he tipped his head to the side.

Shit, shit, shit! I thought that was in my head. Fuck!

"Nothing, forget about it," I responded quietly, desperately hoping he would heed my words and just move on.

"Tell me what you meant." He scrutinized me with his piercing green eyes, doing his best to figure out what my outburst could've been about.

"I said nothing. I mean...I...I don't know what I'm saying. I'm a little out of sorts right now." I'd attempted to straighten my clothes as he continued to peer down at me. Even with my wedge sandals on, I was still significantly shorter than him. I had to change the subject and do it quickly before he probed me any further. "I have to return to my friends now before they send out an APB on my ass. I've been gone forever."

"It's really only been a half hour; you'll be fine." *Is he irritated with me?* Smoothing down my skirt even more, I proceeded to walk around him, trying my best to put distance between us. As I hurried away, I heard him say, "I meant it about your clothes before. You shouldn't choose something so revealing next time."

I stopped short and wheeled around so I was facing him again, almost tripping over my own feet in the process. "I'll continue to wear whatever I want. You can't dictate my wardrobe, not that you'll ever see me again anyway." His rudeness instantly put my guard back up, which was a good thing because I found myself being very careless around him.

"We'll see about that, sweetheart," he said as he brushed past me on his way to the bar.

Yeah, we will *see about that.* I mumbled to myself all the way back to join my friends. When I finally reached them, I saw three guys crowding around my dear roommate and a couple girls trying to swoop in on Matt.

Alexa was in her glory, as usual, but I felt bad for Matt because he looked a little uncomfortable. He was trying to be polite, but the girls weren't picking up on the hints he wasn't interested. *How dense can they be?* He was trying to avoid all physical contact with them, even going so far as shrugging away from them as they tried to possessively grab his upper arm.

I knew what I had to do to save my friend. "Honey, there you are. I've been looking everywhere for you." Making my way past the pushy women, I sat right down on Matt's lap, wrapping my arms around his neck. He was trying to contain his laughter as I leaned in to whisper in his ear. "I thought you could use the help."

"Thanks." It was all he needed to say. Even though I was in the moment, trying to help a friend, I couldn't help but search the crowd around me, hoping to catch a glimpse of the sexy stranger I was entangled with not five minutes before.

My eyes locked with his almost instantly, the snarl on his face suddenly confusing me. *What the hell is his problem?* It was then I caught him glancing from me to Matt then back again. *Oh, okay. Now I understand why he's mad.* Or did I? He didn't even know me well enough to appear to be that pissed off. Yeah, we were pretty intimate a few moments ago, but he couldn't lay claim to me.

I grabbed my watered-down drink from the table and tried to ignore him, brooding glances and all.

I wonder how well the rest of the night will go.

~5~

Alek

Present Day

I should have never walked into that damn flower shop, and I sure as hell shouldn't have bumped into her at the club, ending back up at her place at the end of the night. It took everything in me not to scold her for being so careless, drunk enough to go home with a stranger, even if that stranger was me. But I didn't have a choice. I had to make sure she arrived home safe and sound.

What the hell was I thinking? Distance was the main objective, but I certainly messed that one up.

My one rule.

Never get too close.

Now I'm truly fucked.

Sara was like the sweetest temptation. I knew I should stay away, should engage all of my controls, but in the end, I just needed to have a taste. A taste which would surely undo me.

"Alek. Did you hear me?" Jacinda asked as she raked her finger up and down my arm. She was going on and on about her newest visit to Paris, a trip I couldn't give two shits about. I knew I was being rude, but the woman was forever boring me with her tales. Yeah, I admit it. I slept with her. Any guy would have; she was beautiful. But because she didn't stimulate me, other than in my pants, we only had sex once. And she'd been trying to get with me ever since.

"What?" I distractedly asked, already busy thinking of an excuse to leave.

Instead of taking my subtle hint of annoyance, she decided the best course of action was to try and kiss me. She leaned in and placed her lips on mine. Before she could try and attack me further, I pulled away and took two steps back. "Jacinda," I said, irritation evident in my tone. "I told you, I'm not going there again. *We're* not going there."

"You'll change your mind eventually, baby," she cooed, batting her long lashes at me as she leaned in close again, her breasts rubbing against my arm. "We run in the same circles. I'll wear you down soon enough." She laughed, pecked me on the lips before I could move away and disappeared from my office.

Although I was never going to give her what she wanted, I had to admire her persistence. There were worse things in life than being pursued by a beautiful woman.

It had been three days since I'd left Sara lying in bed, dazed and confused. I'd almost made the mistake of telling her I'd contact her later that day. Thankfully, I'd held my tongue. I couldn't get too close too fast.

I could ruin everything.

Later that night, as I leaned against the shower tile, the hot water cascading over my sore muscles after an intense workout, all I could think about was the woman I'd woken up next to earlier in the week. Her innocence was breathtaking, even more so when she revealed no other man had been inside her. *What can I say? It was a major turn-on.*

Gripping my thick length, I pictured her face when I'd helped her to her feet. Her full, pink lips just about had me marking her right then and there. Beautiful amber eyes stared back at me, full of desire and surprise, but never fear. She stood in front of me in nothing but a damn T-shirt and panties, both doing a shit job of hiding the body underneath. Those memories of her took me to completion, my desire washing away with the water circling the drain.

I knew, right in that moment, Sara Hawthorne was going to be my undoing.

~6~

Sara

It'd been a week since I woke up next to Mr. Gorgeous, aka Alek Devera. An array of emotions conflicted me, streaming through me and confusing me at every turn. I was oddly excited, daydreaming of when I would see him again. If ever. Nervousness raced through me at how much I liked him. I hardly knew the man, yet I felt an unexplainable connection toward him.

His face was the one thing I kept picturing. His voice was constantly ringing in my ears. I didn't like feeling that way, slowly being wrapped up completely in a man. A virtual stranger.

When I finally rushed into our apartment, dropping my keys a few times in my excitement, I threw my things on the couch and called for my best friend. "Lex!" I shouted. "Are you home? Alexa!"

"What the hell are you yelling for? I'm right here." She came barreling out of the bathroom, half-assed wrapped in a towel thinking something bad had happened. That was until she saw my face.

"I got it! My loan was approved for the shop!" I screeched, throwing my hands in the air like a crazy person.

I was beyond words, beaming from ear to ear. It meant more to me than merely owning my own business, which was a huge deal in and of itself. After what I'd been through, I needed this to feel somewhat normal again. *I'll take all of the mundane day to day dealings with owning and operating my own business, the debt which has to be repaid, the long hours to get me started and everything else if it means I have a chance at a regular life for once. Well...in a very long time, anyway.*

I had a normal life once upon a time...before I met *him*. But I won't dwell on the past. It was a happy time for me, and I refused to let anyone ruin it, even myself.

Alexa rushed over and embraced me in a huge hug. "I'm so happy for you, Sara; I truly am. I know how much you wanted this. How many twenty-six-year-old women do you know who own their very own business?" She was smiling right along with me. "I know one. You. When did you find out?"

"I called today on a whim, it being Saturday and all, and actually talked to Mr. Hemsworth, the loan officer I've been dealing with. He was about to leave for the weekend when I caught him."

My cheek muscles started to ache, the stupid grin never once disappearing from my face.

"Did you call Katherine yet and let her know she can officially retire?" she asked as she made her way toward the kitchen to grab a drink. Alexa liked Katherine almost as much as I did, viewing her as the mother figure, just like everyone else.

"No. I thought I would sign the paperwork on Monday, make it legit, and then bring them to work with me. She won't be too shocked, though."

I was excited the plan I'd had for myself was actually going to be my new reality. But to have someone near and dear to my heart express the same type of happiness for my new circumstance was amazing. I truly didn't know what I'd do without Alexa by my side. The gratitude I'd felt toward her was so overwhelming I'd almost been reduced to tears. Thankfully, she hadn't noticed, all too consumed with thoughts of going out that evening and having a great time.

"We have to celebrate. A girls' night out," Alexa sang, dancing around the kitchen island like a woman possessed. "Let's get crazy tonight. I'm sure it'll be the last one for a while since you'll be working like mad in the weeks to come."

She was right. I'd have to buckle down even more and learn the business inside and out. The last thing I wanted to do was ruin all of Katherine's hard work. "Sounds like a plan, but where should we go?"

"There's a small bar called Carlson's about a half hour from here. Some of my co-workers were talking about it the other day. They really like it."

"Okay, we'll head out around seven for an early start to our celebration."

"Sounds good." I'd be able to take a quick nap, run some errands and decide on what to wear. Donning jeans and a nice sweater would be all I'd worry about. Maybe kicking it up a notch with some nice heels.

We arrived at Carlson's closer to eight, a bit later than we had anticipated, but it was okay because we still had the whole night ahead of us.

Although it was nothing more than a corner bar, it seemed cozy and inviting. It was the kind of place you went with some friends to unwind after a hard day of work. A place I could definitely imagine going after a long but rewarding day at the shop.

On either side of the bar, there were numerous high tables, placed a few feet from each other, giving the customers plenty of room.

I liked that not everyone was crowded and squished in like sardines.

"Let's sit over here for now," I said, pointing toward the left corner of the bar which was presently empty.

Once we were situated, my gaze wandered around, checking out the types of people sharing the same space with us.

"What do you want to drink, Sara?" Alexa already had her money out, waiting for my order.

"I guess I'll have a rum and Coke for now. I'll keep it simple."

"Simple? Rum? We'll see how simple that is after a few of them."

Alexa knew me all too well. I was a lightweight when it came to alcohol.

It was ten o'clock before the bar really started to pick up. Before I knew it, it was standing room only. There was a pretty uneven ratio of men to women, men making up about seventy percent. I couldn't care less since I wasn't interested in anyone there, but for Alexa, it was a dream come true. There were plenty from which she could choose. In fact, I think she already had her eye on someone in particular, an attractive blond guy with tattoos running up and down both arms. As he leaned over the jukebox, making his selections, he had no idea he'd just been targeted by my dear friend.

"I'll be right back. You gonna be okay for a couple minutes?" she asked, eyeing me up and secretly pleading with me to say yes.

I laughed. "Go, go talk to him." She hopped off the barstool faster than the words left my lips. She was in full seductive gear: her usual tight, low-cut top and short skirt, paired with the highest heels I'd ever seen. Honestly, I didn't even know how she managed to walk in those things. Her outfit was a bit over the top for a local bar, but that was Alexa. Over the top.

"What's so funny, gorgeous?" *Who the hell said that?* I didn't have to wait long to find out as someone grabbed my arm, whipping me around on my barstool so fast I almost fell off. As I caught myself, I came face to face with a young, dark-haired man, who happened to be very drunk. He was the type of guy you could tell peaked in high school, the popular jock who never went anywhere after graduation. It was probably because those were truly the best years of his life.

In any other situation, I would have thought he was attractive, but not at that moment. There was something creepy and unnerving going on behind those light brown eyes of his.

He instantly made me uneasy.

"Excuse me," I practically shouted, trying to rein in some of my rising temper so as not to cause an unnecessary scene. Even though I was clearly glaring at him, shooting him the worst kind of evil eye, he was still holding tightly. When I tried to shrug him off, his grip only intensified.

"Let go of my arm," I said through gritted teeth.

He looked to where his hand was placed and smirked, slowly releasing his grasp.

"Can I buy you a drink?" He leaned in closer than was comfortable, invading every part of my personal space. The frustrating thing was I couldn't turn back around because his knee was blocking the way.

"No, but thanks for the offer." I was doing my best to remain civil with the creep, but I realized it didn't matter. He was intent on hitting on me, delusional to think I would fall for him in some way. "Can you move your leg so I can turn around now?"

The look on his face was a mixture of shock and anger, because how dare I refuse him? "Why don't you want to talk to me?" He was starting to piss me off the longer it took for him to get the damn hint.

"Because I have a boyfriend and I don't think he would appreciate you hitting on me." It was the only thing I could think of to hopefully placate his incessant behavior.

"Well, where's this boyfriend of yours then? Let him tell me himself I can't buy you a drink."

Is this guy for real?

As if sensing there might be a problem, Alexa came over to save the day. She had more balls than I did when it came to dealing with arrogant drunk men.

"You okay, girl?" Thankfully, she didn't say my name in front of him. I didn't want the creep knowing anything about me.

"This guy won't accept I refused his offer to buy me a drink." *Get him, Lex.*

The dark-haired jerk looked in Alexa's direction, was hit with the sight of her over-exposed flesh and stepped away from me so I could twist back around. I was never so thankful to Alexa for wearing her outfit.

"How 'bout I buy *you* a drink, gorgeous?" Couldn't he think of anything more original?

"Hell no!" Alexa shouted directly in his face. "You stand over here bothering my friend, then offer to buy *me* a drink? Like you're not an obnoxious asshat? Take a hike, creep!" Her temper was rising the more he just stood there.

"Bitches, both of you," he grumbled, trying to steady himself before tripping over his own two feet. He attempted to somewhat compose himself before he walked away, bumping into Alexa's shoulder as he passed by her. I didn't know if it was on purpose or if it was because he was staggering a bit from drinking.

I was praying it was the latter.

"Thank you so much, Lex. That guy was really starting to freak me out."

"I was prepared to punch him if he kept giving you a hard time." We burst out laughing. I wouldn't put it past her to out-and-out deck the guy. We looked across the bar and saw him already back to his antics, trying to chat up an unsuspecting victim. I really hoped she had a friend with her to help her out.

"So...what happened with the hottie at the jukebox?" I tried to distract her enough to stop leering at McCreepy.

My question did the trick.

"Oh, he is quite the hottie indeed. You know I'm a sucker for a guy with tats. He gave me his number and agreed to hang out. I guess I'll call him in a couple days, you know, when I get around to it." She smiled and took a sip of her drink.

Shaking my head, I didn't expect anything less from her. Sometimes I admired her self-confidence and courage. She didn't seem to be afraid of anything or anyone.

I, however, was still re-building my trust in people, forever being the overly cautious one.

It was another hour or so later when we decided to head out and grab something to eat before going home. There was a charming little diner which was open late two blocks away from the bar. We'd only been there a few times, but we always enjoyed the food and appealing ambiance.

"I'm running to the ladies room real quick then we can go," I said as I hopped down from my barstool.

"Okay. I'll be here." She was a little lit-up, but then again so was I. Not drunk, just pleasantly tipsy.

There wasn't anyone in line for the bathroom, so I was able to take care of business relatively quickly. I had only taken a few steps into the hallway when I ran into someone.

To my horror, it was the guy from earlier. "Well, well, well. Look who it is." His hungry eyes slowly cascaded up and down my body. Dressed in skinny jeans and a short-sleeved sweater, he made me feel exposed.

Sucking in a deep breath to try and calm myself before I went into full-on panic mode, I tried to move around him. But he blocked my escape, instead taking a few steps toward me, backing me up against the hallway wall. His hand shot out and grabbed a lock of my hair, yanking me closer. Pain shot through me but before I could scream, his mouth tore at my lips, my sensitive skin pierced from the sharpness of his teeth. I tried to push him off, but my efforts were in vain.

He wasn't budging.

My resistance must have been a turn-on for him, a low groan escaping from somewhere deep in his throat.

It was predatory.

It was dangerous.

Grabbing both my hands and pinning them above my head in one of his, he positioned me right where he wanted me. His free hand lowered until he was pawing at my sweater, trying to grope me. While his body fought with mine, he lowered his head again and tried to kiss me. Again. I kept turning my head from side to side, knowing if his lips touched mine again, I would retch all over him.

"Stop moving, bitch!" he hollered, pinning me harder against the wall.

"Get off me," I yelled, or at least I tried to. My voice betrayed me, coming out as nothing more than a loud whisper. Terrified he would accomplish what he set out to do, I prayed someone would come and save me. Anyone. I just needed someone to round the corner and find me.

My heart hammered away inside my chest, threatening to break free if I didn't calm down. But how could I? I was being attacked, and there wasn't a damn thing I could do about it. Before I was able to try and speak once more, I felt his fingers circle my throat, squeezing until I could barely intake the stifling air surrounding me.

I felt his hot breath on my face, the stench of alcohol making my stomach revolt. "I know you want this. I can see it in your-" He was torn off me before he finished his sentence.

I stumbled quickly before catching my balance. My hand pressed against the same wall I was being held against, trying my best to calm down. When I finally looked up, I saw someone pummeling the hell out of him. It was darker in the hallway than out in the bar, so I couldn't really see who it was. All I could make out was a dark-haired, tall, broad-shouldered man. Other than that, my vision was working against me.

Before I had the chance to leave, I was hoisted onto someone's shoulder then walked through the bar and straight outside into the night air.

Still confused about what the hell was going on, I started to panic all over again, not that I'd really calmed down from a few minutes ago. As my pulse threatened to explode, I was hit with a very familiar smell. Inhaling his sweet scent did wonders for soothing my frantically beating heart.

If I had any doubt who was carrying me, upside-down, I was reassured as soon as I laid my eyes and my hands on his perfect ass. *How can I be turned on so fast by this man when something tragic almost happened to me?*

"Alek! Put me down!" I yelled, surprised my voice was working for me. I was being jostled around on his shoulder, and it wasn't mixing well with my startled mood and the drinks I'd already consumed.

Even though he'd saved me from a dangerous situation, he was still manhandling me.

When he finally put me on my feet, I almost fell. He reached out to steady me but I swatted his hands away. Retreating instantly, he looked volatile. *I don't know why he's so mad.* But then again, I didn't know why I was upset with him.

He just saved me from probably being raped...or worse.

After a few minutes, he seemed to calm down, circling me and drawing my nerves to the surface again.

"Are you okay?" he asked as he continued to lock eyes with me. He had a mixed look of rage and worry on his gorgeous face. I didn't know which emotion was winning out, though.

"Yes, I'm fine," I whispered. Nervously shuffling my feet, I turned my head, looking everywhere but in those mesmerizing green orbs of his. "How did you know I was here?" It was a thought which hadn't occurred to me until that very moment. Instead of thanking him, those were the words which escaped my lips.

"Does it matter, Sara?" *What an odd response.* He started cursing and roughly pushing his hands through his hair, pacing back and forth in front of me, occasionally glancing down to look directly into my face.

I didn't know what to say to him. *Why is this so hard for me?*

"Where was your friend? Please tell me you were at least here with someone," he barked, allowing all of his frustration to come barreling out faster than he could stop it.

"Yes, of course I was here with someone. She was at the bar waiting for me to come back from the bathroom. We were going to head out when that asshole grabbed me." I hated he was making me explain myself, something I hadn't had to do since I lived with my gram. "I guess he didn't like the fact I rejected his offer to buy me a drink earlier."

"You were talking to him earlier tonight?" He was back to yelling again. *What the hell? Does he think I was flirting with that psycho?*

"He offered to buy me a drink, and I refused. There's really not much else to tell. Lex came over and told him to take a hike."

As if hearing her name, Alexa came barreling out the front door of the bar.

"What the hell happened in there?" Her eyes went straight from me to Alek, looking him up and down, taking her sweet-ass time drinking him all in. I knew she couldn't help herself; he *was* quite the sight to behold, broodiness and all.

"The drunk guy from earlier attacked me in the hallway outside the ladies room." I quickly looked away, embarrassment creeping over me again. "Before I knew what was happening, Alek pulled him off me and beat the hell out of him. Then he brought me out here."

Her eyes practically popped out of her head, disbelief evident in her look. She took a few steps closer, reaching out and putting her hand on my shoulder. "Well, he must still be lying in the hallway, because the only commotion anyone saw or heard was you being carried out of the bar over someone's shoulder." She turned her attention back to Alek and just like that, I was forgotten. "Thank God you were here, good sir." She smiled at him and extended her hand. "I'm Alexa. And you are?"

"Alek Devera," he replied, extending his hand in reciprocation.

I looked over as Alexa's eyes widened, her mouth falling open as if she was privy to a juicy secret.

"You're the guy from Throttle, right? The one who helped Sara carry the drinks over to our table?" *Can she be any more obvious?*

"The one and only," he smugly said. I looked from one to the other. *What the hell is going on here? Is she flirting with him? Is he flirting with her?* I didn't think so, but I knew I needed to be alone with him. Right then.

"Lex, can you give us a minute please?" I silently pleaded with her to leave and not cause a fuss. Thankfully, she understood.

"Sure, but I'll be right inside the bar if you need me."

"Thank you." I watched her walk away before I turned my eyes back on Mr. Devera.

I didn't have the chance to utter a single word before he started in on me. "What were you thinking? You should have reported him the first time he bothered you." Anger started to take hold of him again, but I wasn't convinced it was all directed at me.

"I didn't think it was a big deal, just some drunk guy hitting on me. Plus, when Alexa told him off, he stopped bothering me."

"Yeah, look where that got you," he scoffed. "You have to be more careful when you go out, Sara. There are a lot of people out here who will take advantage of you, even hurt you."

He doesn't know how well I already know that last part.

"I know. I misjudged the situation I guess. It won't happen again."

"You're damn right it won't. I won't let it." His breathing had slowed from before, but the look of anger was still very palpable in his stare.

"How are *you* going to prevent it? It was simple luck you happened to be here tonight. Right?" I watched his face, trying to gauge his reaction. "Please tell me it was just a coincidence, Alek."

There was some hesitation on his part before he finally answered. "Yes, of course it was a coincidence I was here. But good thing I showed up when I did or who knows what he would have done to you."

His words made me shudder, even though I had the very same thought not moments before.

Alexa poked her head outside the door again, saving me from saying something I might've regretted. "Hey, I called the cops. They should be here any minute, Sara." Then she went right back inside without giving me any time to respond.

I started shaking my head, not wanting to deal with it anymore.

"You better not even think of not dealing with the cops. You're going to press charges on that asshole." He looked so resolute, I knew there was no use arguing with him.

"Fine, I'll wait for the police and give them my statement."

"And press charges!"

Huffing out a frustrated breath, I responded. "Yes, Alek. And press charges." *God, this guy never gives up.*

~7~

Alek

My heart rammed against my ribs. I was fearful it would never slow back down—not as long as she was in my life, at least. That woman was going to be the death of me. I just knew it. But I wouldn't have it any other way.

Since the very first time I'd laid eyes on her, I knew she was destined to be mine and I would do everything in my power to protect her, even from herself. I'd never experienced any of those feelings before, and I'd had my share of women. There was something about Sara which called to me, beckoning me from afar...and up close. I knew I came off as intense and overbearing, but I wasn't about to apologize for trying to keep her safe.

After she was done speaking with the cops, they went into the bar to escort the guy out so he could tell his side of the story. They found him back in action, drinking, and hitting on some poor unsuspecting woman?

Asshole.

His version of the story was he was going to the men's room and Sara had approached and started kissing him. Then when I showed up and saw them, I lost it.

Sara had to hold me back from pouncing on the bastard right in front of the officers. Both of her hands were on my arm, trying her best to pull me back toward the edge of the curb. I could have easily broken free and tackled the fucker, but I refrained, even though I struggled with my decision. Well, until she rose up on her tippy toes and whispered in my ear, "Don't do it, Alek. I need you here with me."

Her words calmed my struggle, both inside and out.

The police escorted the creep down to the station for more questioning and to let him sober up. They informed us they would get in touch with her if they needed any more information. I had to remind her to tell them she wished to press charges, something I was sure she didn't want to do, but I all but forced her hand.

"Come on. I'll give you a ride home." I laced my fingers with hers and started toward my car, which was parked two spaces down from where we were standing. The ride I'd chosen to bring that night was my black Aston Martin. It was a luxurious vehicle, and once I'd noticed the way Sara looked at it, I knew I'd made the right choice. Even though she tried to seem unaffected by me, I loved the fact I could impress her, even if it was with a hunk of steel.

"I can't leave Alexa here by herself," she mumbled as she suddenly stopped walking.

I blew out a breath of frustration but knew she was right. We couldn't leave her friend there all alone. "Wait here, Sara. Don't go anywhere." My eyes bore into hers, waiting for compliance.

"All right, I won't go anywhere."

Once I knew she wouldn't move, I stalked back inside and quickly located her friend. She was in the corner, busy chatting up some tattooed guy. I should have taken her with us, but I had no right. I hardly knew Alexa, and it certainly wasn't my place to intervene. But I *would* make sure she had a safe ride home when and if she needed it. After I was finished, I walked back outside, locking eyes with my woman. *That's right. Sara is* my *woman, even if she doesn't know it yet.*

When I was within a few feet of her, I reached out and latched onto her hand again, pulling her with me as we walked toward the car. She gave some resistance at first and it confused me. Then it dawned on me I was still manhandling her a little bit. I loosened my grip and waited patiently for her to follow me.

She *was* coming with me. I just hoped she made up her mind before I had to throw her over my shoulder again.

When she still didn't move, I leaned in closer, questioning her with the furrow of my brow. "What are you waiting for?" I asked, impatience rolling off every word.

"What did you say to Alexa?"

I wanted to go, so I blurted out our quick conversation. "I gave her the number to my car service, if and when she needs to use it. Other than kidnapping her, Sara, there is nothing else I can do."

I didn't know if she was trying to compute what I'd said, but I wasn't giving her another second of hesitation. Gently placing my hand on the small of her back, I ushered her toward the passenger side of my vehicle.

When I sensed she was still struggling with her decision to leave, I blurted out, "You're not going back in there tonight, Sara. Let it go." She instantly stood taller, resolve and stubbornness propping her up for a fight. Before she started to argue, I spoke again. "Please, get in the car. It's chilly and I'd like to take you home."

She finally relented and allowed me to open the door for her. Sliding inside, I couldn't miss the look of awe which overtook her. Her head whipped around, taking in every little facet of the car. It was a simple thing, but I'd take it. A big smile broke out on my face as I closed her door and made my way around toward the driver's side.

As soon as I was nestled in, I turned the engine over, the interior lighting up and encasing us both. Pulling out into the street, I breathed a sigh of relief she'd allowed me to drive her home.

"This is a beautiful car, Alek," she said, more on a whisper.

"Thanks. I was thinking about buying a different one, though; I'm kind of bored." Truth be told, even though the car impressed me, which was hard to do, I was getting tired of it. I liked to switch up my rides every so often, a luxury I could more than afford.

Glancing over in her direction, I saw a disapproving look on her face. "What's that look for?" I asked as I found myself shifting in my seat. *Why am I uncomfortable all of a sudden?*

Without looking at me, she muttered, "Rich people."

I couldn't help but laugh. I knew she was impressed with me even though she wouldn't admit it. *And let's face it; it's good for my ego.*

There were a few moments of silence before I broke the building tension. "Why were you ladies out tonight? Anything in particular?" Thankfully, all of my anger from before had finally disappeared.

She answered immediately. "I found out today I was approved for a loan, so we were out celebrating."

"Because of getting a loan?" I chuckled. *What a weird cause for rejoicing.*

My response was obviously the wrong one, instantly putting her on guard again.

"You wouldn't understand because apparently, it's beneath you, not understanding how important this is to someone like me."

She spoke of herself as if she was the lowest of the low, something which I would not tolerate, in any fashion.

Trying to diffuse the situation, I retorted with, "I didn't mean anything by it. Please don't take what I said the wrong way." I reached over and touched her leg and surprisingly, she didn't tell me to remove it. "Explain it to me. Please. What was the loan for?"

Silence.

Unbearable silence.

Finally, after a few very long minutes of her staring out the window again, watching the world go by, she spoke up. "I'm not telling you. Just drop it."

My grip on her thigh tightened a little, letting her know I wanted her to talk to me. Whipping her head toward me, I saw the faintest smile grace her mouth. Even in the darkness of the car, I knew I affected her. She tried to better situate herself, even though I knew she was as comfortable as could be.

I tried to persuade her to answer my question. "Please, tell me about the loan. What's it for?"

"If you *must* know," she started off sarcastically, "it was to purchase

Full Bloom, the flower shop you came into. My boss, Katherine, is selling it to me because she's finally decided to retire. I'm very excited about the transition." Surprisingly, she kept her eyes locked on me. "That's why we were out celebrating. Happy?"

"Actually, yes. I'm very happy for you, Sara. It's a big step owning your own business. I own several of my own, so if you ever need any help, please don't hesitate to pick my brain."

"Why am I not surprised you own many businesses?" Her question was more of a rhetorical one, so I didn't even bother responding.

A few more minutes passed. I was still holding on to her leg, my fingers massaging her thigh. At some point, I guess when she'd had enough, she placed her hand on mine and tried to remove it. I didn't allow her to succeed, though. Not yet.

She stopped fidgeting, but I sensed her breathing had increased.

"Can you please turn the heat down?"

"Sorry, but I don't have it on," I replied, a smirk lifting the corners of my mouth.

"Then can you please remove your hand from my leg?"

What I really wanted to do was move my hand higher up her thigh. Maybe even sneaking it in between. If she'd been wearing a skirt, I might not have been able to hold back, her desire permeating off her, calling for me to claim her in some way.

"Are you sure you want me to? You look like you want me to do other things with my hand."

"I'm quite sure you need to put both hands on the wheel. Right now, please."

I would give her that one, mainly because it was better for both of our safety if I did what she asked. Gripping the steering wheel with both hands did relieve me of some of the torture I had been inflicting on myself.

~ ~ ~ ~

As soon as I pulled up in front of her building, I wasted no time shutting off the engine and hurrying from the car. I could tell she expected me to just drop her off and drive away, but there was no way in hell I wasn't going to walk her inside and make sure she was okay. Especially after what she'd been through earlier.

I'd been to her place before but I'd never gotten the chance to inspect her surroundings and give it my stamp of approval. Glancing around quickly, I gauged the building was one of the nicer ones. But I still wasn't convinced it was safe enough for her. *What are you going to do? Invade her privacy?* Hell yeah, I was. Whenever I was around that woman, all of my sensibility flew right out the window.

She opened her door before I made it over to her side, an action which irked me a little. But I tried not to show it, knowing I was overreacting.

"What are you doing?" she asked as I moved closer. "You don't have to walk me up."

"Yes, I do. After everything that happened tonight, I need to make sure you get inside safe and sound." I wasn't wavering on this. She could fight me as much as she wanted to.

"Fine," was all she said. As we were walking up the sidewalk, I noticed one of the side lights which lined the walkway was out, making it pretty damn dark. I think she knew I was going to comment on it because she tensed up all of a sudden.

"You should really live somewhere well-lit. This isn't safe." I hadn't noticed if she had an alarm system when I was there before but there better at least have a deadbolt.

"It's usually lit up very well. That light must have just burnt out."

"Uh-huh," I grunted.

Once inside, we rode the elevator to the fourth floor. The time spent in silence was a gift since I was trying to calm the rising urge to whisk her away from there.

When we finally arrived, I stepped out after her, the look of disbelief on her face not stopping me. I followed her down the hall and waited patiently behind her as she put her key in the lock.

Once she pushed the door wide open, she turned around and stood there staring at me. "What are you doing? Aren't you leaving now?"

"Absolutely not," I answered as I slowly pushed past her, not waiting for an invitation to enter her residence. "I'm coming in to check and make sure everything is good."

"That's not necessary," she said as she tried to pull me back toward her. "I'll be fine."

Once she realized there was no getting rid of me, she let me go, stepped further inside and closed the door behind us. Thankfully, she was smart enough to leave a light on, so as not to walk in blind. But as quickly as I saw the light, I noticed there was no alarm. My irritation rose, but I tried my best to tamp it back down. I had to approach this with some kind of finesse or I was going to put her off altogether. While I was going to make my demands, they were needed for her security. Even if she didn't agree.

No sense in beating around the bush. "Where's your alarm?" I asked, knowing full well she didn't have one.

"Not everyone has a security system, Alek. We regular folk can't afford stuff like that." Her sarcastic tone told me everything. My wealth bothered her, or at the very least unnerved her.

Ignoring her comment, I turned and started making my way around her small apartment. "That's just careless and asinine."

"We have a secure deadbolt, which is all we need. Plus, this building is one of the safer ones in the neighborhood, so there is no need for extra security."

Ignoring her lame excuses, I proceeded to check the kitchen first before heading down the hall to the bathroom, then each of the bedrooms. Hers was the last one I checked, moving quicker than I knew she could keep up with.

"Why are you checking through this whole place? What are you expecting to find?" she cried out as I disappeared into her closet.

I heard her blow out a frustrated breath and when I finally looked over at her, she was standing tall with her hands on her tiny waist. Her long, chestnut hair was flowing loosely, making her appear even more enticing then she normally was.

She really was quite the beauty, her stubbornness doing nothing to detract from that. In fact, it was making me want her even more. I loved the fact she was a feisty woman, although she was probably less apt to listen to me.

The next few seconds passed as the sexual tension grew between us. Gone was her irritation with me. Instead, she was blatantly checking me out, roaming her eyes up and down my body without shame. It was then I realized I was still standing in the middle of her private space.

There were only a few feet separating us and her bed. Before my mind could wander to the many ways I wanted to take her, I moved a few steps in her direction, holding her gaze with every stride.

A sudden look overcame her, but I couldn't quite make out what it was. *Panic? Confusion?* "Are you all right?" I asked, leaning in closer to check. Hooking a finger under her chin, I lifted her head so she could meet my eyes.

"I'm fine. A little dizziness. No big deal." She looked as if she was going to pass out, her face suddenly very flustered, her breathing faster than was certainly normal. "Are you done with your inspection of my apartment now?"

Taking a step back to give her some room, I answered her question. Although, I was sure she didn't like what came out of my mouth. "I guess so. Everything looks okay, but I'm sending someone by on Monday to install an alarm system."

"What?" she exclaimed, her voice raising an octave. "I don't want you to do that. We're totally fine here; we're safe."

"I won't take no for an answer, Sara. That's final." I knew I was coming across harsh, but I also knew she wasn't going to listen to me if I tried to reason with her. "I don't want to hear one more word about it."

"Yeah? Well, I have *four* words for you, Alek. Get. The. Hell. Out!"

she yelled, emphasizing each word.

Who would have thought behind her sweet persona lay a spitfire of a woman? Not me. To look at Sara, a person didn't always get what they'd bargained for. Not in a bad way, though.

Something told me the more I unraveled, the more intrigued I'd become.

She tried to appear strong, and no doubt she was, but she was also vulnerable.

I saw it.

There's a story hidden behind her eyes.

A dark story.

She tried to hide it with smiles and sass, but it was lurking, struggling to break free given the right, or wrong, circumstance.

I started toward her as if I was intent on changing her mind. "Why do you have to be so difficult? Why can't you do as I ask, without giving me such a hard time?" Standing directly in front of her, my chest lightly grazing her breasts, my whole demeanor changed. She was messing with me, her heavenly scent captivating me and making me a bit dizzy. All I could think about was the way her lips tasted and how much I wanted to bury myself inside her. "You feel it, don't you? This electricity between us?" I didn't give her a chance to respond before I grabbed her face and pulled it upward toward mine.

"Yes, I feel it. So what?" She was trying to seem unaffected but was doing a shit job. I could see it written all over her beautiful face.

Without further delay, simply because she was driving me insane, I covered her mouth with my own. Her soft, warm lips were too inviting and when she gasped, opening her mouth to me, I almost lost it. There was an urgency to our kiss, like we both wanted to devour the other.

Her tongue stroked mine, teasing me as if she couldn't get enough. Her warmth enveloped me, drawing me in closer, tempting my sanity with every lick and taste. Ours was a lovely dance, rapidly becoming something more if I didn't stop it soon. But I didn't want it to end, not yet.

"You taste so good, just like I remembered," I whispered. She groaned, entangling her fingers in my hair, pulling me closer.

I placed my hands underneath her backside, raising her up my body. "Wrap your legs around my waist." I bit her lower lip before plunging my tongue back inside her mouth. For once, she actually did as she was told, wrapping her thighs tightly around me, pushing her core against me.

"Alek," she panted. "Oh...my...God."

I knew I shouldn't have lost control with her but I couldn't help myself. She drew me in and I was powerless to stop it.

Pushing her against the nearest wall, I pressed my body closer to hers, if it was even possible at that point.

Breaking our kiss for the briefest of moments, I encouraged her to put a stop to it. "If you don't tell me to stop, Sara, I fear I'm going to lose all control, throw you down and fuck you so hard, we'll be tangled up in each other for days." I was finding it hard to breathe as my lips cascaded over her throat, feeling her pulse against my lips.

When her response was silence, I broke. Pulling her sweater over her head, I quickly tossed it to the ground, making quick work of removing her bra. Once the clasp was undone, I all but ripped the material from her body, throwing it to the floor, as well. "I can't stand having anything in the way," I groaned as my mouth descended to take her breast, my fingers working on the other, pinching her nipple, working them both until they were pebbled from her excitement. We continued to torture each other, teasing and tasting as if we would never be sated.

As my tongue flicked over her sensitive skin, she cried out, "Don't stop, Alek. Please...I want this." She rotated her hips against me, causing such a friction I almost came in my pants. *Fuck that would be embarrassing.*

I didn't know if it was her words or the fact my reason came rushing back to me, but I instantly broke our fevered connection and placed her on the ground. The look of hurt and confusion on her face almost had me attacking her again. But I couldn't. I wouldn't. I knew she desired me. I knew she wanted me to fuck her, but she was still a virgin and I wouldn't take advantage of her, no matter how hot and heavy we'd just been.

When she reached for me, I backed away, trying my best to hold strong. "No, we can't. I'm sorry, Sara."

"Why?" One simple question, yet I couldn't answer her.

I bent down and retrieved her clothes, handing them to her but avoiding her eyes. I knew the look which was going to be there if I dared to take notice. I couldn't bear to see it so I acted like a coward, avoiding it altogether.

Hearing her inhale a ragged breath killed me. I knew all sorts of crazy thoughts were running through her head and I should have put them to rest, but even I didn't know the right words to help soothe her wounded ego.

Once she was dressed, I grabbed her hand, as I liked to do, and pulled her from the room, walking briskly toward her front door.

"I have to go now, but I'll call you tomorrow. Make sure you lock the door behind me when I leave." Leaning in, I placed a quick kiss on her swollen lips.

Before she could even respond, I was gone, the door closing slowly behind me.

~8~

Sara

It's so dark and cold. Where am I? And why can't I move my arms or legs? I try to open my eyes, but I don't have the strength. What is happening to me?

Suddenly, I hear a noise above me. An old door screeches open as someone starts to descend down a creaky stairwell. Oh, God! What is happening? I try to open my mouth to scream, but no sound will escape.

Then I feel a cold, clammy hand start to caress my face.

Then nothing.

Silence.

Just when I think I imagined someone else is even here with me, I hear him whisper in my ear, "Sara, we are going to be so happy together. You'll see."

~ ~ ~ ~

I was instantly pushed into consciousness, bolting upright and checking my surroundings. I'd been lucky enough not to have that dream in almost five years. Strange it would start up again all of a sudden.

A shower was what I needed, especially since my nightshirt was sticking to me, reminding me no matter how much time passed, I could never fully escape what happened.

I was making my way toward the bathroom when I heard the television on in the living room. I wasn't fully aware of what time it was, but I knew it was quite late. Usually when Alexa came home, she went straight to bed, so I thought it was a bit odd for her to still be up.

As I walked down the hallway a little bit more, she caught my movement out of the corner of her eye and physically flinched in surprise.

"Jesus, Sara, you scared the shit out of me!" she yelled, looking as if she'd seen a ghost.

"Sorry."

"Are you okay?" The more she gazed at my disheveled self, the more concerned she appeared.

"Yeah, just had a nightmare."

"Not *the* nightmare?" Alexa knew all about what happened to me, never judging me or pitying me, just always being my friend, and my best friend at that. Because of everything, she was very protective over me when it came to guys hitting on me, or even just hanging around. Funny thing was, though, Alek didn't bring out that side in her—not that I was aware of, anyway.

"Yeah, but I'm not really up to talking about it. The only thing I want to do is take a shower and go back to bed." I smiled, but it never reached my eyes.

As the hot water rushed over my body, I remembered a time when I was forced to talk about the event. I saw a therapist for about a year after it happened, but all it did was make me relive all the details over and over again. I understood the point of talking to someone when bad things happened, but after a certain point, I was just tired. Tired of dredging up the past, and tired of remembering. So I stopped seeing her long before I moved to Seattle.

Exhausted past the point of thinking anymore, I dried off and made my way toward my bed, curling under the covers and drifting off into a restless sleep.

~ ~ ~ ~

I swear I wasn't asleep more than a few hours when my phone jarred me awake. I heard Mumford and Sons playing as a ringtone. *What the hell?* I didn't put it on there. Reaching over, I snatched my phone from the charger only to reveal the caller.

Alek.

How the hell did he get my number? I never gave it to him. I would have, had he asked, but he never did.

"Hello?" I barely answered, my voice a garbled whisper. *What the hell time is it?* I glanced at my alarm clock and noticed it was only eight o'clock.

"Hi, sunshine. Did I wake you?" The rasp in his voice instantly roused me, doing delicious things to my nether regions. My brain was instantly flooded with images from the night before, making me clench my thighs together to stop the ache before it became too much.

"Um...yeah. You *do* realize it's only eight in the morning, on a Sunday, don't you? Most people are still sleeping."

"Sorry. I wanted to make sure I caught you before you made any plans. I was hoping to take you to breakfast. What do you say?"

How about calling me back at noon?

Instead of refusing, I responded with, "What time are you thinking?"

For some reason, I knew he was smiling on the other end of the phone.

"How about I pick you up in an hour? Does that work?"

I tried my best to stifle my yawn, but it escaped anyway. "Fine, see you in an hour. Do you remember the way here?"

"Of course, see you soon."

Before he hung up, I had one more question for him. "Alek, how did you get my phone number, let alone program yours into my phone with your own ringtone?"

"I have ways of finding out information when I want it." He chuckled. "And I programmed my number into your cell last night on the way home."

I didn't press him further because I knew Alexa gave him my number. I should've been mad at her, but I wasn't.

"I'll be there in an hour. Be ready."

"Okay, I'll meet you out front."

"No, I'll come upstairs. Please don't wait outside, Sara. It's too early in the morning, and you don't know who is out there. Promise me you'll wait for me inside." There was silence on my end for a short time. "Sara! Promise me."

Oh, for the love...

"Okay, I'll wait for you inside. Satisfied?"

"Yes, very. Thank you. See you soon," he said before disconnecting the call.

I swung out of bed and headed toward the bathroom, ready to take yet another shower.

~9~

Sara

It was five minutes to nine when I finished getting ready. I'd thrown on some jeans, boots, and a pretty embroidered white camisole, covered by a royal blue cardigan. A decorative scarf completed the look, plus it would come in handy if the weather was a bit chillier than predicted.

"Sara, Alek is here for you!" Alexa yelled from the doorway of her bedroom. She must have heard him knock and let him in. I wasn't sure why she was up so early on a Sunday. She should've still been knocked out for at least another two hours.

"Be right there." I took another glance in the mirror to make sure I looked presentable enough to be seen in public with the God-like creature who was waiting for me.

I finally made my entrance, trying my best not to keep him waiting. I stopped abruptly when he came into my direct line of vision. He was so damn sexy. It really should be against some law to be out in public looking like that. Exuding limitless amounts of confidence, he was leaning against the island in the kitchen, looking very casual. His hair was behaving in a perfectly unruly yet classic way which suited him to a tee. Something was different about him, though, and it took me but a few seconds to decipher what it was. Moving closer to him, I noticed he was sporting a fresh, one-day-stubble look. That, of course, merely added to his virility. He really was a man's man but with the edge of undeniable elegance. He was both rugged and classy all wrapped in one.

Dark-washed jeans hung low on his hips, more so than should've been decent. His long-sleeve, dark red shirt was fitted to him perfectly—not too tight, but snug in all the right places. There was no missing the fine physique which lay hidden underneath. His look was finished off with dark brown, purposely weathered boots.

I actually felt underdressed, even though his attire was just as casual as mine.

"Wow, you look beautiful," he said, bringing me out of my wandering thoughts.

"Thanks, so do you." *Did I just say that?*

"I look beautiful?" he asked as he cocked his head to the side and laughed. I hadn't noticed until then, but he had a small dimple which adorned his right cheek when he smiled, adding to his amazing good looks.

"You know what I meant." I always became so flustered around him. I had to get better control of myself or I would be in big trouble.

After casually perusing my body, he pushed off the counter and walked toward me.

"Shall we?" He grabbed my hand without waiting for my response and led me out the door.

~ ~ ~ ~

I was thankful I'd worn my scarf because it was a little brisk once we walked outside. But what else should I have expected, being late September in Seattle?

"Where is your car?" I asked as I looked all around.

"It's right over there."

"Where?"

"Right there, Sara". He directed me toward a beautiful pearl-white Audi. A spectacular vehicle indeed. I might've actually liked it better than his Ashton Marvin. Or whatever the name of his car was.

"How many cars do you own?" I asked, lightly running my finger along the side of the beautiful metal. I couldn't even afford to buy one. Well, not yet, anyway.

I'd owned one vehicle in my life, a 1982 Chevy Malibu. I loved that car because I'd bought it with the money I'd earned working many hours at a local bookstore where I used to live. Lasting almost eight years, I'd undeniably received my money's worth.

"I have a few of them. Why, do you like this one?" He was searching my face for a reaction. He didn't have to look too hard, though, seeing as how I was practically drooling over the damn thing.

"It's all right, if you like that sort of thing." I knew I wasn't pulling off aloof very well, but I gave it my best shot anyway.

He wasn't buying it, either. "Uh-huh," he said before opening the passenger door for me.

I had to give it to him, he did gentlemanly very well. When he wasn't manhandling me or teasing me with his mouth, he brought out the big guns with those manners. Someone definitely taught him well.

"I was thinking about going to a quaint little diner off I-90. Are you okay with that?"

"Sure, sounds good to me," I said as I glanced out the window. "I sure hope they make a good cup of coffee. It's the only thing that'll help me function halfway normal this time of morning." Turning my head to face him, I asked, "Seriously, are you always up this early?"

He laughed, as if I was the ridiculous one for not rising at the crack of dawn. "I never want to waste any day, so yeah, I'm usually up this early; earlier, in fact. I actually waited a couple hours before I called you."

Not even knowing how to respond to his crazy statement, I fixated on the world outside again as he drove us to our destination.

We arrived at the diner just after nine-thirty. It was a smaller eatery with only a dozen or so parking spaces surrounding the building. He was right; it was quaint and cozy.

"They have the best veggie omelets here. Do you want to try one?" he inquired as he glanced at me over his menu.

"Sure, as long as they bring the coffee over pronto." I didn't usually eat breakfast, which was a bad habit, I knew. Usually coffee and a quick piece of fruit was all I needed to get me going. But for some reason, my body was requesting I up the ante right then.

After the waitress took our order, we sat there looking at each other. I was by no means complaining, though. *I could stare at him forever, but we should probably talk about something.*

"How old are you?" It was the first question which came to mind, my curiosity shutting down my brain-to-mouth filter.

"Thirty-two. Why, how old are you? Wait, let me guess." He sized me up for what seemed like forever, making me feel a little self-conscious. But the longer he looked at me, the more I had to admit I didn't mind his eyes drinking me in that way. It was as if he was having thoughts which were inappropriate for public.

"Twenty-six," he finally answered.

"Yeah, good guess." I was impressed with his accuracy.

"When is your birthday?" I couldn't stop myself from probing him for more information.

"What is this, twenty questions?" He wasn't offended or irritated by my relentlessness, smiling as if he enjoyed my interest.

"Sorry. It's just I don't know too much about you. Actually, I don't know anything about you except your name, and now your age. Oh, and that you have remarkable taste in vehicles." I really needed to get my hands on his Audi. *I wonder if he would let me drive back to my apartment.* He struck me as someone who liked to be in charge, so I couldn't really picture him in the passenger seat of any car.

The backseat maybe, but not the passenger seat.

"Fair enough, I guess. My birthday is in October." Deciding it was an informative back and forth, he asked, "When is your birthday?"

I learned long ago not to give out too much personal information about myself to people I didn't know, but for some reason, I had an innate feeling of security toward him.

Before I could utter the words, he caught me off-guard when he uttered, "September."

"What?"

"I'm guessing the month you were born. September." *Wow, this guy is good.*

"You guessed right again. You must have a gift."

Before he could respond, the waitress brought our plates over, interrupting any further conversation we were about to have.

I didn't realize how hungry I was until she put the hot food down in front of me. Diving right in, I had to control myself so I didn't appear like a homeless person eating for the first time in a week.

"Anything else you want to know?" he asked between bites of his omelet. If possible, I think he was even hungrier than I was. But then again, I was sure he needed plenty of nourishment to keep his glorious body in working condition.

I pondered my next few questions. He'd given me the perfect opportunity to find out more about him and I made sure to take it.

"Have you always lived in Seattle?"

"Born and raised," he answered, a dreamlike look on his face as he continued talking. "Most people hate the weather here. They just can't get used to the rain. But I don't mind it. Not at all." He took a sip of his water before speaking again. "I guess I'm used to it. Frankly, I can't see myself living anywhere else." His smile was huge, his fondness for his city was apparent. "What about you?"

"What about me?"

"What made you move to Seattle?" he asked, shifting in his seat as if he'd known he'd asked a sensitive question.

'What makes you think I wasn't born and raised her as well?" My eagerness to end our line of questioning was starting to weigh heavy on me. I knew I'd started it but I wanted to be the one to end it. Soon.

'Trust me, I would have known if you grew up around here." He leaned forward and reached across the table, brushing his hand over mine. The contact only lasted for a split second but it was enough. "I would have met you a long time ago."

His words struck me like lightning. I'd known the man was interested in me but the look he gave me made my body light up from the inside. It was as if he was peering directly into my soul.

A shiver ran through me, making me jerk back and garnering a startled look from him. "Sorry, I must have gotten the chills."

"Would you like a jacket? I have one in my car." He had no idea those weren't the type of chills I'd been referring to. But I wasn't going to elaborate. My body twitching uncontrollably, if only for a second, was not something I wished to explain over breakfast.

When silence pressed the space between us, I knew he was going to ask his question again.

"So, what made you move here?" he repeated.

I wasn't sure how much information to reveal so I kept it short and sweet. Well it started that way, at least, morphing into a full-blown point-by-point as the minutes ticked by.

"One day I decided I wanted a fresh start. Thankfully I wasn't alone, Alexa promising to follow me anywhere. Wherever it was I wished to move. So one day she pulled out a map, told me to close my eyes and point." His eyes widened the more I'd spoken. "As you can see...I pointed to Seattle."

I'd tried not to read into his expression too much. I chalked up his astonishment to having a hard time believing I'd thrown caution to the wind, uprooted my life and relocated across the country. All from a dare to blindly point at a map, my future depending on luck of the draw. What if I'd chosen Alaska? I wouldn't have done so well with the extreme cold.

"Can I ask you another question?"

He nodded. A simple gesture giving me the opportunity to find out even more about the man sitting across for me.

"What do you do for a living?"

I caught him right as he put a forkful of food in his mouth so he raised a finger, signaling for me to hold on so he wouldn't answer with his mouth full. I nodded and continued to gracefully devour my meal.

"I own a few businesses here and there." He continued to eat his omelet as if his answer was going to placate my curiosity.

When he didn't elaborate further, I continued to press him. "Really? That's all you're going to give me? It doesn't tell me anything."

He shrugged and bit his lower lip. He was acting like he didn't want to divulge too much information about these *businesses*, and I wasn't quite sure why.

As I parted my lips, he gave me something. "My grandfather left me an inheritance when he died. He actually left it to both me *and* my sister, but in the end, I received it all." He trailed off toward the end of his story, looking past me as if he was lost in thought.

"So, you have a sister?" *Why do I get the impression I shouldn't push this topic?*

"No, not anymore. And I don't want to talk about it." A glaze had washed over his features, as if he was containing the urge to shut down completely. There was no mistaking his demeanor had changed to one which was standoffish.

"Ok, you don't have to talk about anything you don't want to. I was only trying to get to know you a bit more, that's all." I was really okay with whatever information he wanted to share with me.

"You'll have to forgive me. There are certain things I refuse to discuss with anyone. Please don't take it personally, Sara." He gave me that dazzling smile of his, immediately putting me at ease.

I was never quite sure how to act around him, different emotions bombarding me all the time. One minute, I felt as if I was walking on eggshells, and the next, I was trying to curb an emotional outburst of his. Then I was rendered breathless and begging for his touch. I'd never felt like that with anyone before in my entire life. Not even close.

"So, as I was saying, I received an inheritance from my grandfather when he passed away. I used some of the money to buy a hotel, which I later turned into two, and so on and so forth. In less than a decade, I was able to turn them into the largest chain of hotels on the West Coast." He took a bite of his toast before blurting out, "Oh, and I also own a few nightclubs, Throttle being one of them."

I almost choked on my food, what with all the information being spewed at me in the matter of thirty seconds.

"Anything else?" I was merely being sarcastic at that point.

"Nope." He smiled. "I think that's it." He continued eating as if what he'd revealed to me was no big deal. And to him, I was sure it wasn't. But to me...it was a little overwhelming.

He was in mid-chew when he glanced at me. I must have looked a certain way because after he swallowed his food, he put his fork down and interlocked his fingers, resting them casually on top of the table.

"Are you okay? Does any of that bother you?" His question was genuine.

"No, it doesn't bother me, per se. I'm a little surprised is all." My face reddened after a simple thought crossed my mind. "There I was going on about my excitement over a little flower shop and here you own *everything*."

I was intimidated. I could admit it.

"You had a goal of owning the shop, Sara, and you saw it come to fruition. It's a great accomplishment; don't ever forget that. And hey, at one time, I only owned *one* hotel." He winked as he polished off the last of his meal.

After a few more intense, quiet moments, he shuffled around in his chair, settling in and getting more comfortable. Taking a sip of his water, I could do nothing but watch the way his throat worked at swallowing the cold liquid, his tongue tempting me as it slid over his lips.

"Sara? Did you hear me?" he asked as I finally raised my eyes from his delicious mouth to his dark green eyes.

Oh, shit! I totally didn't hear a word he said.

"I'm sorry, what did you say?" A low groan of embarrassment

erupted, spurred on further by his faint laughter.

"I asked you about your family. Are you close with them? Do you have any siblings?" He raised the glass to his mouth once more, and I had to restrain myself from getting lost in the pure sight of him again.

"Sorry. Um...I...don't have any family," I stuttered. Blowing out a quick breath of air, I continued divulging my story. I was going to do it quickly, however, because just as he didn't want to talk about his sister, I really didn't want to talk about my family, or lack thereof.

"My father died when I was very young, still a baby. My mother called it 'an unfortunate accident.' He was an abusive drunk who came home one night, starting up with my mom about something insignificant and stupid as usual, and tripped over his feet, hitting his head on the edge of the coffee table. He died instantly." *I can't believe I just blurted all of that out.* I was usually very protective about my past, but with him it was as if I had no worries.

I kept going. "I only have a few memories of my mom growing up, but the one which really sticks out is my fifth birthday party. It wasn't anything fancy, only my mom and a few of my friends, but I remember being so happy that day, my mother's smile etched forever in my brain." Looking away to regain some of my fleeting strength, I turned toward him again. "I only have a few memories because she passed away when I was eight years old. She was coming home from work one night and was involved in a head-on collision with a man who had suffered a heart attack, killing them both instantly."

Hearing him suck in a breath almost undid me. Tears had been building and threatened to spill over if he did or said anything overly sentimental.

"Who did you live with afterwards?"

Relieved he didn't delve into anything too deep, my emotions started to retreat enough for me to finish. "I lived with my grandmother, Rose. She became like my second mother. I think we helped to heal each other to get through the tragedy. After all, I'd lost my mother and she'd lost her daughter." I vanished in my own thoughts for a minute, tearing my eyes away from him and staring at my trembling hands. Finding one more ounce of strength, I pushed through, wanting to finish this and move on. "She passed away a little over a year ago, and I still miss her like crazy every single day." My retreating tears were back in full force, ready to make an appearance any second. "Can we talk about something else, please?" I begged, hoping he would change the topic as I'd done for him earlier.

"Sure thing, and thank you for sharing with me, Sara." He didn't say much more, smiling as I gazed over at him. I weirdly felt closer to him, as if my story was building a stronger bond between us. I always felt physically safe when I was around Alek and at that point, I was starting to feel emotionally safe, as well.

As we were preparing to leave, I picked up the check to see what my half came to. Withdrawing money from my wallet proved to be the wrong thing to do, a disgruntled look appearing on his face as he ripped the bill out of my hand.

"What the hell do you think you're doing?" he asked, a semi-scowl still set in place.

"I was seeing how much I owed for my breakfast. Why? What's the problem?"

I didn't think he knew the proper reaction one should have had to my simple gesture. Was he accustomed to people using him for his money, always expecting him to pay for everything? Because that wasn't me. I always paid my own way. *Always.*

"Put your money away." *Is he insulted?* "I think I can cover breakfast, for Christ's sake."

"Are you angry I offered to pay for my half of the bill?" I was going to make him explain his outburst.

"No, of course I'm not angry. Sorry, I just don't want your money, ever. I'll always take care of things when we're out together, even when we're not. If I feel you need or want something, I'll make sure you have it."

Wow, where the hell is this coming from? I loved the fact he envisioned us out together in the future, but I didn't want him to feel as if he had to take care of me.

"I won't give you a hard time about buying me breakfast, but that's it, Alek. You are not buying me anything else or paying for me when or if we go out anywhere else. I can pay my own way, thank you very much. Plus, it's insulting if you think I can't take care of myself. I've been doing it for quite some time."

I was the one who was becoming miffed by the second.

"I didn't mean to insult you, Sara. It wasn't my intention." He reached across the table and touched my hand. "But I won't waver on this."

I wasn't going to argue with him anymore. It wasn't the time or place. "Can I at least leave the tip?" *Wrong question.* He gave me an even more annoyed look, furrowing his brows and huffing out an aggravated breath.

Holding up my hands in submission, I said, "Okay, okay. Sorry I asked."

He paid the bill and we left the diner, his hand resting low on the small of my back. It never failed; every time he touched me, even in the most innocent of ways, I started to feel all woozy and warm, even in the early Sunday morning hours.

As we walked toward his car, I blurted out my approval again over his mode of transportation. "I really love this car. It's so beautiful."

He gave me a look as if he was the cat who ate the canary. *Oh, no, what is he thinking? Wait, I* know *what he's thinking.* "Don't even think about it, mister!"

"What? I don't know what you're talking about." Grinning, he opened my car door for me, not elaborating or continuing our short conversation.

~10~

Alek

The drive back to her place was excruciating. I wanted to spend more time with her, but I also didn't want to rush anything. Although, at the same time, I did. I'd never been so conflicted before in my entire life. Feeling like I'd known her forever was simply the tip of the iceberg. The more she chose to share with me, the more she drew me in, even if I'd shut her out earlier by not talking about my sister.

I just couldn't.

It'd been years, but it was still too soon.

I heard her breaths, coming short and quick beside me. Confused as to what had caused the change, I turned my head slowly to face her. What I saw almost made me swerve off the goddamn road. Her eyes locked on me, her tongue darting out every now and again to moisten her lower lip. *Oh, how I want to bite that lip.* When she saw I was looking, she quickly turned away, flustered she had been caught leering at me.

"Did you want to ask me something, Sara?" I inquired, knowing full well words had indeed escaped her.

"What...uh...no...no," she stammered. I couldn't help the laugh which erupted, knowing exactly how she felt. My own heart was hammering away inside me, but I was much better at controlling my emotions. Although, I was finding it difficult the more time I spent around her.

I was going to tease her, but we arrived at her place faster than anticipated. Turning off the engine and exiting the vehicle, I made my way to her, opening her car door before she could do it for herself. Knowing she was annoyingly independent, I thoroughly appreciated she allowed me the simple gesture. It meant something to me. I was a firm believer in men opening doors for women, carrying their things for them and catering to them, within reason. I wanted a woman who could take care of herself but chose to let me do it instead.

Sara was one such woman. She was strong in her own right; I knew that much about her. And I knew it was going to be difficult for her to let me take charge, the small incident with the bill an indication. I didn't want to boss her around or control her. I only wanted her to listen to me, to allow me to take care of her.

It was hard to explain, but in my head it all made sense. *Now I have to find a way to make her understand.*

Slowly but surely, she will come around.

I reached for her hand to help her from her seat. Closing the door, we slowly walked to the front of her building, her palm still clasped in my own.

She stopped by the front door, fiddling with her scarf. "Well..." she trailed off, never finishing her thought.

"Well, what?" I pushed, knowing she was a bit flustered once again. I loved the affect I had on her; my ego stroked with every whimsical glance she cast my way.

"Thank you for breakfast, Alek. I'll talk to you later?" She was asking me, as if she didn't already know the answer.

"I'm not going anywhere until I make sure you get inside, safe and sound."

"Alexa is still home. Do you honestly think there is someone hiding in our apartment? With her in there? Because I can tell you this much: she would do some serious damage if anyone tried to break in while she was there." A small smile played on her lips as she tried to remain serious.

Placing my hand over my heart, I tried pleading, something to which I certainly wasn't accustomed. "I don't doubt that, but for my sanity, can you please allow me to walk you inside? I promise I won't search the whole place like last time." I winked as I finished my sentence, hoping she would relax a little and give in.

After a few very long seconds, she relented. "Fine."

"Fine," I mimicked as I followed her inside. Once we stepped into her place, I had to remind myself of my promise not to go searching through every room looking for intruders. I took one step too many into the living room when I heard a loud rush of air behind me.

It was her.

Her sigh none too quiet.

Clearly, she was frustrated.

Clearly, I was the one trying her patience.

"Alek," she said in warning.

"Sara," I replied, my brows knitted close together. My faux seriousness was enough to pacify her, her facial features relaxing almost immediately.

"Well," she mumbled, shifting her weight from one foot to the other. "Thanks again for the omelet."

I couldn't help myself, forever wanting to garner a reaction from her. Taking a step closer, I circled my hand around her waist and pulled her into me. She stumbled before placing her hands on my chest. "There was coffee, as well," I joked, leaning down until my lips were dangerously hovering over hers.

Her breath fanned my face, warm and sweet. So enticing.

"Thank you for the coffee," she panted, our closeness causing her quick breathing.

My hand tightened, bunching her shirt in my fingers. "And there was toast." My tongue licked at her bottom lip, teasing the hell out of both of us. If I wasn't careful, I would be the one walking away tortured and bruised.

Her gasp almost undid me, inhaling a piece of my soul as she swallowed her breath.

Her words were soft, like a whisper in the wind. "Thank you for the toast."

Since I couldn't think of anything else we had eaten, I closed the remaining distance between us, pulling her so close her breasts touched my chest. I tangled my hand in her long hair, gripping it so she couldn't move. When my lips finally descended onto hers, the mixture of our breaths fueled our rush of desire.

I knew I should have just walked her inside, said my goodbyes then left. But something about her always messed with my reason, and I was treading dangerous territory lately. Her small moans, her need to devour me, and her willingness to give herself over to me in that moment were winning out over any amount of sensibility I should have possessed. Her tongue stroked mine, dancing and playing, until all of my thoughts were of getting her naked and fucking her senseless.

We were so caught up in our rapture, neither one of us heard when Alexa came into the room. I wasn't sure how long she'd been standing there, but once she made a small coughing noise, we broke apart.

Instantly.

Regretfully.

Sara seemed to be somewhat embarrassed, but me? I couldn't give a shit. I didn't care who saw what the woman reduced me to. Nothing more than an overactive hormone.

"Sorry to interrupt. I just need to get a drink," Alexa whispered as she brushed past us and walked toward the kitchen. I looked down to see Sara's reaction but she was watching her roommate, waiting for her to get whatever she needed and leave us. Alone. To continue torturing one another.

"Continue." Her best friend laughed as she walked back down the hall, disappearing into her bedroom.

Sara locked her fingers behind my neck, caressing the back of my head. Pulling me toward her again, I knew exactly what she wanted. But I was done. Her friend interrupting us was exactly what needed to happen; otherwise, we would've been there all goddamn day. As much as I didn't want to leave her, I actually had some shit I had to take care of.

Unlocking her fingers and taking a few steps back, I reached for the door handle behind me. "What time will you be home from work tomorrow?"

"Why?" she asked.

"Because someone has to be here when the alarm company installs the system."

She furrowed her brows and pursed her lips, clearly not happy with my answer.

"Alek, I told you—" she started to say, but I cut her off immediately.

"Don't even try it. You're not going to give me a hard time about this. Your safety is my number one priority. Plus, it'll ease my mind tremendously." I reached out and grabbed her hand, softly running my thumb over the top of it. "You don't want me to worry every second of the day, do you? And you want your friend to be safe, as well?" I knew I wasn't playing fair, but whatever it took. Right?

I could see the struggle happening within her. She didn't want me to purchase something she surely thought was unnecessary and elaborate. But she was also contemplating the safety issue, knowing full well the alarm would put her own mind at ease. Just when I thought she was going to argue with me again, she huffed out a pent-up breath and simply replied, "Fine. I'll make sure someone is here so they can install it. Happy?"

"Very. Thank you." I took one more look around her living room/kitchen before locking eyes on her once more. "Okay, I'll give you a call tomorrow to see how everything went." Leaning in, I gave her a quick kiss before opening her door and disappearing down the hall.

I fought every urge I had not to run back in there and throw her down on the couch and take what was mine. My hand shot right to my pants, trying to calm the raging effect she had on me.

Soon.

I would finish what we'd started very soon.

~11~

Sara

"Hey, where did Alek go so soon?" Alexa asked as she walked toward me, her eyes looking all around our small space.

All I could do was stare at the door, wishing he didn't have to leave. "He had to go."

She exhaled a quick whistle which caught my attention. "You're one lucky girl, Sara. That man is unbelievable. How did you get his attention? Share your secret with me. Please. I beg of you." Her laughing was covered by the sound of clinking dishes. Alexa was always scurrying around for something to eat, but for the life of me, I had no idea where she put it.

"I really don't know, to tell you the truth. He came into the shop one day and has been showing up ever since." A small smile tickled my lips, the mere thought of him too much to contain any sort of straight face.

"Well, you're super lucky. And I'm not ashamed to tell you I'm jealous, you lucky bitch." I laughed at her outburst as I made my way toward my bedroom to gather laundry.

~~~~

The rest of my day flew by, but not quick enough to keep my thoughts from reverting back to Alek every couple minutes or so. I found it hard to concentrate on anything Alexa said, not even feeling a little guilty about it either.

We ended up hanging out and watching *Vertigo*, an old Hitchcock movie, but I couldn't fully concentrate on that, either. My thoughts kept creeping back to the feel of his hands on me, of his perfect mouth covering mine and his enthralling smell which would forever draw me to him.

I went to bed a few hours later, my thoughts still wrapped around him and wondering when I would see him again. I didn't like the feeling of desperation, but I was powerless to control it.

Part of me wanted to escape the desire growing inside me for him. Another part wanted to throw caution to the wind, along with my emotional well-being. *Just go for it*, I tried to convince myself. *Ride out whatever this is until he undoubtedly loses interest.* Not a good way to think, but it was inevitable. Right?

~~~~

As I lie here, tied up and unable to move, my panic overwhelms me. The more I inhale the air in the room, the more I'm suffocated with the awful smell surrounding me. I'm bathed in complete darkness, so terrified my body is frozen in fear, the deafening silence almost too much to bear. As I focus on the sounds of my shallow breaths, I hear it—the frightening sound which tells me he's near. The creaking stair means the man who has altered my world is descending in order to get to me.

I wait.

And wait.

But nothing.

The sound stops, the silence pounding in my ears until a scream gurgles deep in my throat, threatening its escape as I continue to lie here in my own despair.

As my pulse slows, I feel it.

A cold hand caresses my cheek, and before I can allow my scream to tear through me, his fingers circle my throat, tightening his grip until I feel faint. Dizziness takes over until I slip deep down into the bliss of unconsciousness.

Clutching at my throat, I shot up in bed, sweat coating my entire body. *Why is this dream threatening me again?* The faint light from the bathroom crept under my door, allowing my vision to adjust to the darkness quicker than normal. My eyes roamed around the room until I deemed there was no imminent danger. I was safe. My breathing slowed to normal, my heart following suit. When I laid down, fully calm, I tried to fall back asleep, praying my nightmares wouldn't return for another visit.

~ ~ ~ ~

My alarm blared into the silence of my room at seven o'clock the next morning. Although I'd planned on getting an early start, my dreams had kept me up most of the night. Turning toward the offensive noise, I clicked the off button and laid there, my smile so big I knew it was going to be a good day.

I was going to tell Katherine the good news, even though she told me all along everything would work out.

For the both of us.

I arrived at the shop a half hour before we opened. Katherine had already given me a set of keys, so I set about getting ready for the expected busy day.

Matt was the first to arrive after me, which wasn't unusual—always the early bird and all that. At first glance, he looked tired, dark bags hiding underneath his eyes. Actually, he looked like shit the closer I moved toward him, but I wasn't about to call him on how disheveled he looked.

"Hey, Matt. How was your weekend? Do anything exciting?" I asked as I prepared the order slips for the day.

"Not too much, just hung out with some friends. You know, grabbed something to eat and had a few drinks." Snatching his water bottle off the counter, he tore off the cap and drank half of it in a few long gulps. "I had a good time but nothing crazy to rehash." *Somehow, I doubt that.* "How about you?" he questioned, finishing his drink.

An instant blush crept over my cheeks at the memory of Alek. I wouldn't go into any details with Matt, even though he was my dear friend. "No, nothing too exciting here, either."

We exchanged guarded smiles and returned to getting ready for the day's work.

A half hour later, Pete came in. Katherine wouldn't be there until the afternoon due to a few appointments, so I guessed I'd have to wait to share the good news for a little while longer.

I almost blurted out my excitement to Matt a few times but ultimately kept my mouth shut.

"Pete, do you know how many deliveries we have today? I think I'm missing a slip or two. Do you see anything back there?" I called from the front of the store. The shop was on the smaller size, so I didn't have to raise my voice too much for him to hear me back in the prep room.

"Yeah, there's three slips back here. I took them since I was going to deliver them first. Sorry about that."

"No worries, just glad you found them."

Katherine made sure to have all of the arrangements made up before she left on Saturday. *I really don't know what I'm going to do without her expertise. But I guess it's time for me to start learning as much as I can while I still have full access to her brilliant, artful mind.*

Thankfully the hours passed by quickly, taking us a little past lunchtime. I wouldn't have even known what time it was except my stomach decided to make the loudest noises ever.

"Little hungry, are you?" Matt teased as he walked past me, smiling then going on about his business.

I was freaking starving. I couldn't believe I'd forgotten to bring something to eat. In my excitement to get there, I didn't even think about it.

As I was about to call in an order, Katherine came walking into the shop carrying a bag full of takeout.

"Anyone hungry?" she called out.

Saliva instantly coated my tongue, the aroma wafting through the air. "Oh, my God, you are such a lifesaver. I'm beyond starving." Hastily grabbing the bags, I ripped one of them open and grabbed the first thing I saw. The wrapper from a turkey panini was no match for me. The sandwich was hanging from my mouth as I made my way to the tiny break room.

Matt and Katherine laughed at me as I put the other bags down, rounding the table to take one of the two empty seats.

"Looks like I arrived just in time," she joked as she removed a salad. Matt was chomping away on a turkey club, a satisfied grin on his face with each swallow he took.

"Yeah, I'm famished today for some reason." After taking a few swigs of my water, I decided it was as good a time as any to spread my good news. It was perfect since we were all together. "Oh, hey, guess what?"

Instead of saying anything, both of them looked over in my direction, brows raised and waiting for me to spill it.

"I got the loan!" I exclaimed, my lunch fully finished and tossed in the trash.

"That's fantastic news, Sara!" they chimed in together. I knew it wasn't a shock to either of them, but their excitement was genuine.

"I'm thrilled for you, honey, and rest assured, I won't go until you're comfortable running everything. You know I wouldn't leave you high and dry." Her nurturing smile put my sudden nerves at ease. I was really going to miss seeing her every day, when the time came for her to leave.

"I really appreciate it, Katherine. More than you know."

She reached over and patted my hand before making her way toward the prep room.

As Matt and I were getting ready to go back to work, I heard the bell ring above the front door, indicating someone had walked into the shop.

"I'll take care of them, Matt," I said, knowing full well he would rather work in the back than deal with the customers. He wasn't anti-social by any means; he simply preferred the quiet over the constant chit chat from the people who stopped in.

Coming down the hallway, I stopped short as soon as I saw who was leaning against the coolers. I'd just been with him the day before, yet the effect he had on me was as if I was seeing him for the very first time.

His presence was simply mesmerizing.

He looked super yummy in a beautiful dark blue suit. His stark white dress shirt a nice compromise to the all-over dark color; his grey-blue striped tie brought the whole outfit together.

My God, he was beyond sexy. I didn't know how he was able to walk out in public without getting mobbed by women. *Oh, why did I have to go there?* He probably *was* mobbed by horny women everywhere he went. I instantly felt jealous, all over fictional bitches clamoring and vying for his attention.

His movement pushed me out of my own head. Walking toward me, his heated gaze made me dizzy roving over me from head to toe. Slowly. When his beautiful green eyes came to rest on my face, it was then he chose to speak, his sultry voice washing over me like a dream.

"How are you, Sara?"

Great, now you're here.

"What are you doing here?" I blurted out, not even considering how rude my question was.

He didn't bat an eyelash. "I stopped by on my way to a meeting to remind you about the install later today. They're coming at seven. Who's going to be there, you or Alexa?"

How many damn times is he going to remind me about the install? "I'll be home by then, so it's not a problem."

Before we could continue our conversation, Katherine joined us in the front of the store, Matt following behind with a large arrangement in his hands.

Alek smiled in Katherine's direction but when his eyes landed on Matt, his expression faltered, becoming somewhat rigid. He didn't like my friend. It was written all over his face. I knew it didn't have anything to do with Matt personally, instead having everything to do with me. Or whatever relationship he thought we had. Little did he know he had nothing to be worried about, my dear friend preferring the company of men to women. But it wasn't my place to tell his business, so until I deemed it pertinent, I was keeping my mouth shut.

The awkward silence was stifling. I'd lost all sense of manners, staring at my friends and totally ignoring Alek. When another minute passed, he reached out his hand and introduced himself to Katherine first.

Real smooth, Sara.

"I'm Alek Devera, a friend of Sara's. Nice to meet you." Smiling at the old woman was going to surely cause her to faint right in front of all of us.

I saw her visibly falter as she held his palm in hers, thinking God knew what. "Hello, Alek. Pleasure to meet you. I'm Katherine," she said before taking a step to the side and pointing at the other man in the room with us. "And this is Matt."

The two men shook hands, eyeing each other up before releasing their grip. Alek was clearly sizing up his *competition*, Matt returning his scrutiny. I think I was the only one who realized what was happening, all the more reason I was becoming very uncomfortable.

"So tell me, Alek. How do you know our Sara?" Katherine questioned, clearly interested in the new man in my life, even if she thought he was only a friend.

"I came into the shop last week and have been lucky enough to hang out with this beautiful woman a few times since then." *Short and to the point.*

"I see." Katherine's sudden curtness had me knitting my brow in confusion.

As if he sensed something wasn't quite right, Alek politely excused himself. "Well, I should be going now before I'm late. Nice to meet you all." He turned toward me and asked, "Sara, can you please walk me out?"

It wasn't a request.

I moved toward him and he instinctively gripped my elbow, helping to usher me from the shop. I normally would have taken his actions as possessive but truth be told, I didn't mind—not from him. I was thrilled each and every time he thought to touch me, even in the most innocent of ways.

Once outside, he escorted me further down the sidewalk, away from the big window of the store.

Figuring we were in a more private spot, away from any potential roving eyes, he stepped closer. "I'll call you later tonight." It was all he said before he leaned down and kissed me. It was a simple, soft kiss at first, but the longer his lips covered mine, the more sensual the entanglement became. He started invading my mouth, searching for my tongue to entertain his own. Our display was not fit for public consumption, but I didn't care. Any reservations I would have had completely disappeared with every stroke of his kiss, every graze of his lips and every breath we shared.

Raising his hand to grip the back of my neck, he accidentally, or purposely, grazed the side of my breast. The look on his face gave nothing away, but it didn't matter; he was going to drive me crazy, right there in the middle of the sidewalk in broad daylight.

Suddenly, he broke the kiss, leaving me wanting more. I was sure it was his intention all along. His gaze lingered on my mouth until he eventually connected with my eyes.

He was grinning. Big.

"Are you happy with yourself?" I panted breathlessly.

"Why, yes, I am." He was still smirking as he walked toward his car.

Katherine was patiently waiting for me when I finally made my way back inside. I was unknowingly running my fingers across my lips when I saw her, staring at me with a questioning look in her eyes.

"What?" I asked, baffled by the expression on her face.

"Honey, do you know who that is?"

"Yeah, Alek Devera." *Hello? You just met him.*

"How do you *really* know him?" I wasn't sure I knew exactly what she was asking me, my impatience for this whole dance quickly irking me.

"I met him when he came into the shop, just like he mentioned. I've run into him a few times since then." I didn't get into any of the specifics with her; I wanted to keep those private. Plus, I didn't even know where to begin or how to explain our encounters.

Coming out from behind the counter, Katherine took a few steps until she was standing beside me. The look on her face was shock mixed with wariness. "He is *the* Alek Devera. He owns half of Seattle and then some."

"Yeah, I found out all that yesterday." There wasn't much more to say other than that.

"Be careful, honey. He has quite the reputation, and I would hate for you to be swept off your feet, blindsided by his charm, and of course those looks of his. But then again, who could resist that face?" she said, more to herself than to me. "Oh, if only I was about forty years younger..." She trailed off as the corners of her lips turned up, meeting her eyes immediately.

Her outburst had us both laughing, and it felt good to release some of the tension which had been building since he'd walked through the door.

"But seriously, be careful with him."

"I will. We're only friends anyway, so it's no big deal," I lied. I wanted to protect my secret a little while longer.

~12~

Sara

Katherine's outburst about Alek had me wanting to do some research of my own. I had to see what I was in for if I was going to continue to entertain the idea of seeing him again. Utilizing the computer at the front desk, I made quick work of it since I didn't want to tie it up for too long.

Searching for the name 'Alek Devera' instantly bombarded me with image after image of the man who sent my heart aflutter. Most of the pictures were of him with a woman. So many different women. My excitement fell the more I saw, inexplicable feelings of jealousy coursing through my veins. After my eyes had enough of the barrage of pictures, I couldn't decide which was worse: the fact he was always with a different woman or that he couldn't settle on just one.

Nevertheless, he always looked stunning, ever the photogenic subject. Most of the images looked like they were from some sort of fundraiser or charity type event, the formalwear a sure giveaway.

Mixed in with the formal pics, there were some candid ones, as well. Walking out of a building, getting into the back of a town car and even strolling along while talking on his cell phone were among the many other images ingraining themselves into my brain.

When I finally peeled my eyes from the pictures, I read some of the articles. He was very involved in numerous charities, but the one which he seemed to be the most active with was for domestic abuse.

Out of all the causes in the world, why this one?

When I came across some clippings mentioning his philandering ways, I almost stopped my search altogether. But of course, my curiosity won out, needing to find out as much about Alek as I could. *When is Seattle's most eligible bachelor going to finally settle down? Who is the woman on his arm this week? Is Alek Devera seeing two women at the same time?* Those were the types of articles I came across, aggravating me more than should have been normal.

Maybe Katherine was right. I should be careful with him. Maybe he had his own agenda for wanting to see me. Maybe he was only trying to get me into bed, seeing me as a challenge because I was a virgin.

No matter how much I tried to reason with myself, I couldn't stop myself from finding out.

~ ~ ~ ~

I made it home in time to meet with the install guy. He was in and out in record time, going over all the instructions before he left. Admitting I felt safer was almost like admitting defeat; that Alek really did know best. But I wouldn't dwell on it too much, realizing the sense of security his generous offer provided was long overdue.

"Sara, your cell is ringing. Do you want it?" Alexa called out from the kitchen.

I knew exactly who it was from the ringtone. "Let it go to voicemail. I'll get it when I'm done changing." I wasn't planning on going anywhere for the evening, so my normal protocol was to change into PJs for the night.

My phone instantly started ringing again, went to voicemail then started ringing again.

Man, is he persistent.

The fourth time my phone rang, I picked it up.

"Are you okay?" he blurted out before I could even say hello. "I was worried something happened to you." His tone confused me. He seemed irritated but also genuinely worried, for what reason I had no idea.

He just had someone install a high-end security system. What the hell does he think would happen to me in that short amount of time?

"I was busy, Alek." My curtness came out more stern than I planned but maybe it was for the best, letting him know I was a grown-ass woman who didn't answer to anyone.

"Too busy to answer your phone?"

"What did you need, Alek?" I asked right away, wanting to get to the point of his call. I was weirdly flattered he was worried about me, but he was going about it all wrong.

"I'd like you to answer the phone when I call you," he demanded. After a few moments of silence, I parted my lips to respond with a smart-ass comment but he cut me off before I could speak. "Please," he beseeched, his tone softer than before. I heard a twinge of desperation in his voice and it confused me.

If I agreed with him, he'd move on. So that was exactly what I did.

"Fine, Alek. Fine," I huffed into the phone, so ready to change the subject.

Pleased with my response, he jumped right into it. "So, now that the installation is done, are you all clear on how to use the system? Have you ever had one before? Do you know what to do? Does Alexa? I have the same system, so if you need any help, I can be there in no time at all."

Jesus, he didn't even take a breath. His verbal spewing had me smiling—until a certain thought occurred to me. *How did he know the install guy was gone?* Oh, good Lord, he was unbelievable. "Did you have him call you when he finished the job, Alek?"

"Of course I did. Why, does that shock you? Because it shouldn't." I heard him chuckle, relieving some of the tension on his end. Or was it on my end?

"No, I guess not," I confessed.

It really didn't.

"So, are you okay with operating it?"

As I was describing my comfort level with the complicated piece of equipment, I heard a knock on the front door. "Hold on, someone's here."

My fingers circled the knob and I tugged it open, not even really paying attention to who it could have been.

I sucked in a rush of air when my eyes landed on the man crowding the entryway, looking even more delicious than he had earlier in the day. Alek didn't even wait for me to invite him in, instead taking a few steps forward, brushing past me as he entered the small but comfortable space.

He was still dressed in his fancy suit, his tie a little lopsided from a long day at the office. I didn't think I'd ever tire of seeing him dressed that way. Although he made casual look just as sexy. Actually, he looked even better practically naked, a memory forever etched into my brain.

So, in essence, no matter what he was wearing, or *not* wearing, he was still drool-worthy.

"How long have you been standing there? And why didn't you tell me you were on your way over?" It was then I remembered I was in a tank top, braless nonetheless, and small jersey shorts. My pajamas.

He took his time perusing my body, making me blush profusely for some reason.

"I just pulled up, and I didn't tell you I was coming over because I didn't want you to try and talk me out of it. I needed to see you." Taking another quick glance up and down my body, he took a step closer, both fists clenched at his sides. "Why would you answer your door dressed like that, Sara?" The air between us instantly shifted to an uncomfortable one. He was actually pissed off.

He really was unbelievable. I thought women were the only ones with those kinds of mood swings.

Defensively, I put my hand on my hip, trying my best to keep the sarcasm from my voice. "Well, the only person who would come by to see us would be Matt. So it's perfectly fine I'm dressed this way."

Apparently, it was the wrong thing to say. His nostrils flared, and his jaw clenched so tightly I thought it would shatter from the sheer pressure alone.

"You fucking dress like that around Matt? I can see your tits straight through your tiny-ass shirt. And those shorts are clinging to every part of you." Realizing he was almost shouting, he took a deep breath before continuing. "I'm doing everything in my power not to drag you into your room and rip off what little clothing you have on. I can only imagine what runs through *his* head when you dress like this." He was fuming, pacing back and forth in front of me. "Do you want to fuck him, Sara?"

I hadn't been around Alek all that much, but it was the most he'd cursed in my presence and the fact it was in anger, directed at me, was throwing me off.

It was a good a time as any to tell him Matt was gay, but I didn't want to. It wasn't my place to tell anyone, but he was leaving me no choice. I really didn't want him to think there was anything going on between us. The unnerving need to tell him was becoming too much.

"It's not a big deal, Alek." Sensing he was getting ready to yell again, I quickly interrupted him before he could utter another word. "He's gay. Matt's gay, Alek, so there's nothing for you to be worried about. He couldn't care less if I answered the door naked, although that might embarrass the both of us." I was trying to make light of the situation, but I could see by his expression he wasn't amused.

Not in the least.

Damn, Mr. Temperamental is really in a mood.

Daring to crowd his personal space, I courageously took a single step in his direction, his demeanor softening the closer I moved to him. I was still unsure of his mood so I stopped there, close enough to gauge his curiosity but far enough to retreat if I had to.

"You still shouldn't be dressed like that in front of anyone, Sara."

"Even you?" The words left my lips before I'd realized what I'd said.

"Especially not me. Not if you want to preserve your innocence," he confessed, trying to disguise the look of want hiding behind his beautiful eyes. He huffed a quick breath and stalked toward me, looking as if he was going to pounce if I didn't take cover.

His movements forced me to retreat, slowly making my way toward the kitchen. Our eyes locked on one another, his smoldering gaze almost too much to bear. He was telling me everything and nothing at all. Desire was clear in not only his face but the rise and fall of his chest. The curve of his mouth and the sight of his tongue teasing his bottom lip were driving me insane.

His mere presence ignited my desire. What would happen when he actually touched me?

It wasn't until my back came flush with the kitchen island did I stop moving. Before I could even attempt to turn away, he wrapped his arms around my waist and hoisted me on top of the counter. Moving his strong body between my thighs, he pushed my scantily clad legs apart to fully accommodate him. His thick arousal pressed tightly against the seam of his pants.

I was lost.

Lost in what I'd fantasized about since I'd met him.

Lost in the dream of it all coming true.

Lost in...him.

Working his hands up from my waist, he brushed his fingertips over my sensitive nipples, hardening them at once.

"Alek," I pleaded, the mere thought of what was to come making me squirm where I sat, imprisoned in his lustful hold.

"I tried, Sara. I really did," he whispered quickly before he leaned down to capture my mouth. His kiss wasn't gentle. It was deep and hungry. He was desperate to taste me.

To own and claim me.

I didn't resist him, not at all. Snagging my lower lip, he dragged the sensitive flesh through his teeth, causing me to lose all control. Completely and utterly. I wrapped my legs around his waist and pulled him closer.

He had one of his hands firmly placed at the nape of my neck, almost as if he was holding me in place so he could continue his assault on my slightly bruised mouth. His other hand lowered until he grabbed the waistband of my shorts. Pulling the fabric away from my belly, he slid two fingers down until he found my clit.

He broke our kiss, moving slowly toward my ear, nibbling at my skin until he landed on my lobe. "Do you want me inside you, Sara? Do you want to feel me stretch you? Tell me you can't wait for me to fill you"—he bit the sensitive skin—"with my thick cock."

What the hell could I say to that? *Yes, please* sounded too polite. What I wanted to scream was *Hell yeah, I want you to fuck me into the middle of next week.* But those weren't the words I chose. Instead, a simple "Yes" escaped my lips. I was hoping he knew what that one simple word really entailed.

Every stroke from his fingers made me so dizzy, I couldn't even think straight. I wanted to order him to take me to my bedroom and have his way with me, but I couldn't get the words out. I could only focus on what he was doing to me, right there in the middle of my apartment.

My hands lifted upwards until they were tangled in the thick mane of his dark hair. Gripping him hard, I pulled his lips to mine once more, making it so we were devouring one another.

His hand was still expertly working on me, bringing me closer to orgasm. I moaned into his mouth, pleading with him to continue until my body exploded. "That..." I panted. "That feels incredible. Don't stop. Please..."

It wasn't until he pushed inside, my walls gripping his fingers, did I build toward my release. His thumb feverishly worked my clit as his fingers stretched me, the feeling strange but amazing.

I matched his rhythm with my thrusts, building and building until my muscles finally clenched, giving way to the most intense orgasm of my life.

"That's it, baby. Come for me." He continued commanding my mouth, his tongue teasing me as I rode out my high.

When the pleasure started to subside and my breathing slowed, the haze which had been built up around me dissipated, throwing me back into the reality of the situation.

Withdrawing his hand from my shorts, he grabbed me by the waist and lifted me down until my feet met the ground, my legs a little wobbly still. I instantly clutched onto his arms, doing my best not to topple over until I'd regained all of my strength. He held me tightly, giving me the time I needed.

No sooner had we let go of one another did Alexa come walking down the hall toward the kitchen. Toward us. She stopped abruptly when she saw the flushed look on my face. Quickly looking up at him, I couldn't help but notice how calm he seemed. And dare I say unaffected?

"Am I interrupting something?" she asked, having the decency to actually blush, stopping in her tracks and looking to me for approval to approach further.

"No, it's okay. You can come in and get whatever you need. Don't mind us." I was trying to control my flustered voice as I spoke to her.

She smiled and said hello to Alek as she passed by. Once she was hidden behind him, she found my eyes and mouthed *holy fuck*, making me laugh at her brazenness. Alek gave me an inquiring look. I shook my head and laughed again.

He ushered me from the kitchen and toward the front door. *I guess he's leaving now.* Trying my best to hide the look of disappointment on my face, I looked up at him and gave him a genuine smile.

"Well, I better be heading home. I have to go out of town for a couple days, but I'll call you when I get back." He reached out and grasped my hand. "Please answer your phone, Sara."

When I didn't respond right away, he cocked his head to the side and gave me an expectant look. *He'll wait here all night until I give him the answer he wants.*

"All right already, I'll answer your call," I said with a smirk.

"Okay, make sure. And hit the code to the alarm as soon as I leave." He leaned closer and gave me a sweet goodbye kiss, never giving way to what had occurred a few feet away a couple minutes before.

Then he was gone. And I was left already missing him.

Oh, this can't be good.

~13~

Alek

I'd never been so happy for a business trip before in my entire life. My short time in Vegas would hopefully help me to get my head on straight again. I was weakening around Sara and plainly put, it wasn't fucking good.

I tried over and over to take it slowly, to try and get to know her and give her adequate time for her to get to know me in return. But every time we shared the same space, all of my reasoning simply disappeared.

Daily meetings and countless hours of dealing with the construction plans for my newest hotel were enough to keep me distracted. It was only at night, when I was alone in bed, did my thoughts drift to the one woman who turned my world upside-down. I'd thought I was immune to feeling that way, but I guessed I was wrong.

And I was never so happy.

Still, we *were* moving a bit fast. Not for me but certainly for her, I was sure. I needed her to trust me completely. I needed her to never doubt my genuine feelings for her because if she ever found out what I was hiding, I needed her loyalty and unguarded love to help her see the real me again.

It was Thursday evening when I finally called her.

"Hello." She answered on the second ring. I think she was trying to go for nonchalant, but she didn't quite pull it off. I knew she was as excited to talk to me as I was to her, although *I* was able to hide the eagerness from my voice.

"Hi there, beautiful. Miss me?" I couldn't help myself, forever wanting her to stroke my ego. Among other things.

"No, not particularly."

I decided to call her bluff. "Now why are you lying to me, Sara? Do I have to put you over my knee and spank the truth out of you?" I heard her gasp, a sound which instantly had me rock-hard. The image of her bent over my knee was torture, but her response to my outburst almost made me lose it.

"Do what you think you have to, Alek." There was no shyness in her reply, which I found kind of surprising seeing as how she blushed quite a bit when she was near me. *I guess that's the beauty of the phone.* She could be as brazen as she wanted in the privacy of her own home, far away from my prying eyes.

"Don't tempt me, Sara."

A few seconds of building tension was all she needed to switch the subject. "So, how was your trip? Did you take care of whatever it was you needed to?"

"There's still a pressing matter but nothing I can't handle." Work was the last thing I wanted to think let alone talk about, but I didn't want to discourage her from asking me questions about my job.

"Well, I'm sure everything will work out fine." She was silent for a moment. We both were.

I didn't know why I was suddenly nervous. I wanted to ask her to come over for dinner Saturday night, but the fear she could say no was something I didn't want to think about. In reality, I knew she would say yes, but there was always the small chance she could decline and that would crush me. I acted all cool and collected in front of her, but inside I was freaking out. Well, not freaking out, but nervous nonetheless.

Diving right in, I threw out the invitation, hoping she would accept. "Sara, would you like to come over Saturday night for dinner? I'm cooking," I said, patiently waiting for her reply.

Thankfully, I didn't have to wait too long. "Yes, of course. What time?"

"How about we make it for seven o'clock? I'll make sure you have the directions." I hoped she didn't think I was an ass for not picking her up, but I had a surprise for her. A surprise I was sure she was going to give me a hard time about, but I would persuade her to see it from my point of view, like I always did. "Until then. Goodbye, Sara." I hung up before I lost all my willpower, drove over to her place and pinned her against her bed.

The thought alone was enough of an image to pleasure myself to later on.

~14~

Sara

I was so busy at work the next day I didn't really have an opportunity to dwell on thoughts of seeing Alek on Saturday. I was beyond excited but nervous, as well. My body's reaction to him was so powerful I could only wonder if we would end up in bed together. My first time. Normally, I would have been anxious, but the thought of Alek being the man who would claim my innocence set off an instinctive need to surrender to him.

He was the only man I'd let inside my guarded bubble.

He was the only one who had ever made me feel safe.

After the initial rush had calmed down later in the afternoon, I grabbed my phone to check and see if I had any texts or voicemails from him. *A girl could dream, right?* As I opened it up, it rang. I answered immediately.

"Hey, girl. What are you up to tonight?" Alexa asked.

Trying to hide my disappointment it wasn't Alek, I answered nonchalantly. "I didn't have any plans. Why? What were you thinking? Movie night?"

"No, I was thinking more like going out for a drink. Since we both have work early tomorrow, we won't stay out late. I promise." When I didn't answer right away, she pleaded with me. "Pretty please with sugar on top? I've been stressing badly at work and I need some liquid relief."

Deciding to put my friend out of her misery, I agreed. "Okay. As long as we're not out too late, I'm good with a quick drink. I'll ask Matt and see if he's free, yeah?"

"Yeah, of course. Sounds good. I'll see you at home later."

~ ~ ~ ~

We all decided to go to a well-known, local watering hole. It was a pretty big place but it wasn't overly crowded, which was probably due to the fact it was a week night.

Once we had our drinks in hand, we found a private place to sit so we could just chill and hang out.

"So, what's going on at work, Lex? Are the women there driving you crazy again?" I knew she had some issues with some of her co-workers but normally she didn't let it get to her, choosing to ignore them and go on about her business instead.

"No, this time it isn't about the women." She gazed out toward the crowd, not really looking at anyone in particular but instead, staring out into thin air. I bumped her shoulder with my own, nudging her to tell us what the problem was at work. "It's the new boss," she finally confessed.

She had mentioned to me once before the marketing firm she worked for was recently bought out. Now, apparently, she didn't like who was in charge.

"What's wrong with the boss?" Matt chimed into the conversation.

"Well, for starters, he's unbelievably hot," Alexa grunted.

"Why is that a problem?" Matt and I amusingly said at the same time, which only made us laugh harder, gaining a faint smirk from Alexa.

"It's a problem because I can't fully concentrate on my job when he's loitering around next to me. I feel inadequate when he asks me a question and I have to have him repeat himself. Then there are times where I swear he's considering firing my distracted ass. All of it has made for a very stressful situation over the past few weeks."

She took a long drink after spilling all her information.

Matt wrapped his arm around her shoulder and pulled her close. "You have to figure out ways to steer clear of him then. Do you sit close to him? If you do, can you request to move your office somewhere else?"

"His office is at the far end of our floor, so asking to move would kind of seem ridiculous. And it's not like I see him all day long, but when I do, I can't control my wandering thoughts." Slumping forward a little, she continued with, "I just have to suck it up and get over it. Somehow."

"I'm sure you'll figure it out, Lex. Plus, it's not the worst problem to have at work. A hot boss? We can all only dream." I tried to make her see there were worse things which could happen in the workplace. Having someone nice to look at wasn't really one of them.

"I have a hot boss," Matt commented, which made us all laugh.

"Yes, you do, my friend," I replied, flicking my hair over my shoulder.

As I turned my head while goofing off, I caught a glimpse of Alek standing near the bar. *I wonder what he's doing here.* It was weird to find someone like him in such a casual place. The shock of actually seeing him took a few seconds to wear off.

As I contemplated walking over there and saying hello, I saw a blonde woman shimmy up next to him, running her hands all over him as if they were a couple.

My heart sank.

I knew we weren't exclusive. Hell, we weren't even dating, but the sight of him with someone else was too much.

Trying to convince myself to play it cool, I looked away from the offensive sight and turned back toward my friends. *Don't think about him. Don't you dare think about him.* But I did. I did think about him. How could I not? He'd consumed my every thought recently. And there he was, across the bar, with some beautiful...bitch. *Yeah, I know. I'm being catty, but as long as I don't voice it, it's okay. My secret is safe with me.*

My thoughts were interrupted when Matt nudged me. "Isn't that Alek over there, Sara?" He leaned closer to get a better look. "Who's the woman with him?" he asked, continuing to stare.

"Yeah, it's him, and I don't know who she is." I tried to appear unaffected, but inside I was a wreck. "If you guys will excuse me, I need another drink. I'll be right back." I was sure they could see I was upset.

Sneaking through the crowd so he wouldn't see me, I found a place on the opposite side of the bar. Luckily, I was able to get served upon arrival, nursing my drink while I thought about what I should do. Should I say hi? Should I make him introduce me to his *friend?* Should I ignore him? Damn it! I had no idea. My heart beat fast as I tried to decipher which emotion was actually plaguing me.

Anger?

Heartache?

Jealousy?

A mixture of all three?

I wasn't in my seat two minutes when I heard his voice behind me. Because my mind was all over the place, I never even thought to keep an eye out for whether or not he actually saw me.

"Don't you think you've had enough to drink, Sara?" he asked as he reached across me and tried to push my drink away. His scent enveloped me, making me think all sorts of crazy thoughts. Squaring my shoulders, my body went rigid as I slowly turned around in my seat. I couldn't let on to the effect he had on me. I was too upset.

I guess I'm settling on the emotion of anger.

"I can take care of myself, Mr. Devera. Thank you very much. But if you insist on feigning interest over someone, why don't you do it with your date?" I huffed, pointing toward the woman who was all too happy rubbing against him.

"Who exactly are you referring to?" *He knows exactly who I mean.*

"The woman who has been hanging all over you. The one who obviously thinks you're an item," I snarled, anger sneaking out on the tip of every word.

I turned back around and reached for my drink, but he was much quicker than I was. He abruptly grabbed it and handed it off to the bartender before I could utter my objection.

"Alek, what the hell? You can't possibly think you can stand there and dictate how much I'm allowed to drink. You have absolutely no right and you know it." He had such nerve, toying with me, pretending to be interested in me, even inviting me to dinner at his house. Then showing up with some other woman.

I knew us running into one another was a coincidence, but still.

"I have every right since I seem to be the only one who is constantly looking out for your well-being."

"Oh, okay," I scoffed. "Yeah, I'm really in an unsafe place right now, surrounded by all these people. Not to mention my friends are with me. Get over yourself."

I motioned for the bartender, waiting for him to make his way over. I wasn't going to let him get away with treating me like I was some stupid female who couldn't handle her liquor. Admittedly, sometimes I became a bit tipsy, but if I wasn't driving, what did it matter? I didn't drink much to begin with, so I didn't see the harm in letting loose every once in a while. *I can't even believe he's making me justify wanting a drink, to myself nonetheless.*

"Like I said, go control your date's every move...not mine."

"She is not my date!" he barked. I'd obviously wormed my way under his skin. *Good.* It was the least I could do given the shitty circumstance.

He calmed down right away, running his fingers up and down my arm. "I only have eyes for you, Sara. Don't you know that by now?"

"Go sell that crap to someone who will believe you, Alek." My statement made him wince.

I shrugged my arm away from his touch, burning a hole right through the back of the bartender. I'd never wanted a drink more than I did at that exact moment. I needed it to calm my rising nerves, but I also wanted it simply to aggravate Alek.

Finally, the bartender made his way back over but before I could give him my order, Alek told him to cut me off, informing him I wasn't allowed any more to drink. The bartender simply nodded. "Sure thing, Mr. Devera. Whatever you say."

I turned around so quickly, I smashed right into him. *Damn, can't he give me any room?* "You're such an arrogant ass," I mumbled through clenched teeth. "What gives you the right to cut me off? I've only had two drinks so far tonight. That's far from being at the point where you should be concerned, not that you should even *be* concerned about what I'm doing." Admittedly, I was allowing my emotions to take over, reacting more dramatically than I would have with anyone else.

It's all his fault, really.

The bastard actually smiled at me. Ugh, I had to get away from him before I really snapped out and lost it. I wasn't a violent person, not by any means, but I was struggling with not throat-punching him right then. I tried to wriggle free of my seat, but he blocked my escape.

"Move," I said, a little too calmly. I was trying to rein it in, no matter how hard it was. I put my hands on his chest, trying to make him back up, but he didn't move. Not one step. He laughed at my feeble attempt, stepping even closer than he was before.

"I'm not going anywhere and neither are you, Sara. Not without me, at least." As he was about to reach for me, the woman who had been rubbing against him earlier saddled up to him, seized his hand and attempted to pull him close.

At first glance, she was a very attractive woman, her long, blonde hair trickling down her back in large waves. Her model-type figure instantly made me self-conscious, her pouty lips the final blow to my self-esteem. But the more I looked at her, the more I could tell she was someone who was only concerned about herself. Fakeness crept from every pore in her perfect body.

"Who do we have here?" she asked with reserved contempt, checking me out from head to toe. She tried to pull off sweet but failed miserably.

"Apparently no one," I retorted. As Alek turned his head to look at her, I knocked him off-balance enough to take a step back. It was all the room I needed to escape. And escape I did. Quickly. I ran through the place looking for Alexa and Matt. I knew they were there somewhere, but it was hard to peer through the sea of people.

"Sara!" Alek yelled behind me, his voice too close for comfort. I broke out in a run, dodging in and out of the other patrons, still searching for a glimpse of my friends. *Oh, where are they?*

Finally, I saw Matt standing in the far corner, talking to a very handsome guy. They were standing a little too close, but not enough for anyone to think they were anything except good buddies. But since I knew his secret, I saw what was obvious to me.

I hastily made my way over to them. "Matt, are you leaving anytime soon?" I was out of breath but I didn't want to alarm him, trying my best to calm down as quickly as possible.

"Yeah, I was about to head out in a few minutes. Why? What's wrong? You look like someone's been chasing you." *He hit the nail on the head and he doesn't even know it.*

"No, I was just flustered because I couldn't find you guys." I broke eye contact with him and scanned the area near us. "Where's Alexa?"

"She's somewhere out on the dance floor. You know her; a good song is all it takes." He reached for my hand and pulled me into him, suddenly glancing from me to the guy standing on his other side.

I nudged him. Hard. "Introduce me to your friend."

"Oh, sorry. Sara, this is Marcus. Marcus, this is my dear friend, Sara."

"Very nice to meet you, Marcus." He was very attractive, not as handsome as Matt, but pretty darn close. His ashy-blond hair complemented his light brown eyes. He actually reminded me of the boy next door but with some sex appeal.

We were engaged in light conversation when I felt someone tug on my arm. Glancing over, I saw Alek standing behind me, crowding my personal space.

"Can I have a word, please?" he asked, trying to appear calm, but I saw the cracks in his appearance. I could see right through his façade and it made me smile...on the inside, of course. I was happy to see I'd had a profound effect on the infuriating man.

"No. I don't have anything to say to you, so you may as well leave." I stood firm, my resolve unshakable. Okay, it was shakable, but I tried very hard to pull off the opposite effect.

Completely ignoring me, he grabbed my hand and tried to tug me away from Matt—who, by the way, was in the crosshairs of Alek's dangerous scowl. They clearly didn't care for one another. Matt didn't trust Alek, for reasons unknown to me. And Alek wasn't fully convinced Matt didn't want to sleep with me. The thought alone was absurd. He had no romantic feelings for me at all, but there was no getting that through Alek's thick skull.

"Five minutes. Please, Sara," he implored, which I found surprising coming from a man with his type of power and wealth. I couldn't imagine him even *asking* for the attention of the opposite sex, let alone trying to convince them to be alone with him.

When he didn't let go, Matt felt as if he should step in on my behalf. "She said no, Alek, so why don't you get lost?"

Oh, no!

"Well, Matt, this is none of your business. This is between me and Sara. I'm warning you. Don't interfere." He was quite literally glaring at Matt, tempting him to make a move.

"You're warning *me*? Who the fuck do you think you are?" Matt yelled as he advanced toward him. With my eyes practically bugging out of my head, I sucked in a quick breath, glanced from one man to the other, and put myself smack dab in the middle of them.

"Who am *I*? I'm the guy who's gonna kick your fucking ass if you don't mind your own goddamn business." He was practically spitting at Matt, so I knew I had to act quickly. I put my hands up and gripped his upper arms to try and get him to back up. *Holy shit*! He was even more defined than I remembered; he would surely hurt Matt if it escalated any further.

Although Matt was fit, muscular and could hold his own, I was sure he was no match for Alek. The man was not only taller than Matt, but he was physically bigger and would surely put a hurtin' on him. I didn't want any of that to happen. While I'd appreciated Matt sticking up for me, I didn't want him to be put in the position of defending me.

"Alek, come on. You wanted five minutes? I'll give you five minutes, but you have to move. Now!" I practically shouted in his face. His icy stare slowly shifted from Matt to me, his face gradually changing when his eyes connected with mine.

As we were walking away, I heard Matt yell after us. "This isn't over, Devera!" I knew Alek heard him because he sucked in a breath and made to turn around, but I grabbed his hand and pulled him toward the front door.

He nearly crushed my fingers, letting up some when I smacked him on the arm. "Is it your intention to break my hand?"

"Sorry. I just love the feeling of touching you. I get a little overexcited, I guess," he confessed, smiling at me. You would never know he'd almost been involved in a fist fight a minute ago. The man was the master at switching moods when it suited him, which could be somewhat dangerous, depending on the situation.

I let go of his hand when we reached the sidewalk and saw his face fall, although he recovered quickly.

"You would be wise to tell Matt to back off in the future, or next time there won't be any warning."

"Matt was only trying to protect me. You of all people should understand that. You should be grateful I have a friend who cares enough about me to stick up for me, especially against a crazy man such as yourself." I tried to get him to see how ridiculous he was being, but I probably wouldn't convince him.

"I will admit nothing. And I'm still not convinced he doesn't have an ulterior motive, Sara."

"Alek." I sighed. "I'm not going over it again. I told you before. Matt is gay. Please, let it go already," I huffed. The look on his face was truly priceless. *I'm sure he's not used to having people dismiss him. Ever.*

"We'll see." His eyes flicked all around, taking note of our surroundings before shifting his penetrative stare in my direction.

"So, what's so important you had to cause a scene? What did you want to talk to me about?" I asked, kind of already knowing what he wanted to discuss.

"I wanted to make sure you knew I didn't come here with Jacinda. I know what it must look like, but I swear there's nothing between us. I'm only interested in you, Sara. Please, trust me."

Trust you? Well, maybe don't let another woman grope you.

"Did you ever sleep with her?" *Oh, my God, I can't believe I just asked him that.* He'd probably tell me no, though.

Without missing a beat, he answered. "Yes, but it was a long time ago." *Okay, I didn't see that one coming, but at least he's being honest.* Although, I then had a picture in my head of the two of them rolling around naked, and it started to make me see red.

Which led me to my next awful thought. Why was he pursing me when he could just as easily hook up with her? Anyone could see how much she wanted him.

"Well, she obviously wants you. So...uh, why don't you leave me alone?" He managed to fluster me, making me trip over my own damn words.

Narrowing his eyes, he bit his lower lip and tried to come up with something to say in response to my little outburst.

"Are you jealous, Sara? Are you jealous of Jacinda?"

What the hell? Is he mocking me?

"Of her? Really? Be jealous over someone who is so obviously fake? I don't think so!" I exclaimed, and quite loudly, too. I knew I was being petty, but I didn't care.

"You're right. There's no need to be jealous of Jacinda. No need at all."

Stop saying her name!

"But she obviously wants you, Alek," I repeated. "Try and deny it."

"I'm fully aware she wants me. But *I* don't want *her.* I want *you.* It's as simple as that. I thought you knew this already."

The words came out before I could stop them. "Why would you want me when you can have her?" *Shit! I can't believe I asked him another stupid question.* Nothing like putting it out there how vulnerable and insecure I was.

When he didn't respond, I forced myself to look up into his gorgeous face, the square of his jaw ticking as if annoyed. Would he all of a sudden realize I was right and he should be with her? Would he instantly become aware of how ridiculous it was to chase someone who fought him at every turn? I didn't know, but I hoped not.

With every fiber of my delicate heart, I hoped not.

After what seemed like forever, he finally broke the silence. "Why would I want someone like her when I have someone like you? You're the total package, Sara. Don't you see that?"

I was stunned.

Truly stunned and a bit confused.

"You are beyond beautiful and have a body which makes me want to lose my mind every time I have the pleasure of looking at it, let alone touching it. You're a strong woman who is not afraid to speak your mind, ever. And although you are the most obstinate, exasperating woman I have ever met, you make me feel things I've never felt before, not with anyone. So again, I ask you, why would I want someone like her, or anyone else for that matter, when I have someone like you?"

He was holding my chin up toward his face to make sure I could see the sincerity in his eyes.

Without letting another second pass, he pulled me into his embrace and proceeded to kiss me with a passion which should've only been reserved for private. But I gave in to him because I couldn't hold back any longer, either. His arms snaked around my back and gripped my shirt, trying to pull me impossibly close. It wasn't until I released a small moan into his mouth did he really unleash his possessiveness toward me. His tongue invaded my mouth, trying to claim every piece of me. His dominant ways were evident through his kiss and I found myself loving every minute of it.

We were sadly interrupted when Alexa and Matt came bustling outside looking for me. It *was* getting late, and I had a busy day ahead of me at the shop. Shuffling his feet near the entrance to the bar, Matt kept his eyes locked on Alek, glancing over at me every few seconds to make sure I was okay. Alexa, on the other hand, had an ear-splitting grin plastered on her face. When she caught my attention, she winked and made an O face. She actually made me laugh. She was so brazen, not caring what anyone thought, which made her actions funnier to me.

A few seconds of awkward silence followed. "Well, I guess I should be going now," I said, taking a step back. A step he clearly didn't like, but there wasn't any more we were going to do that night. I had to go, and he knew it.

"Can I give you a ride home?" he asked as he invaded my personal space again.

"Thanks, but I came here with my friends and I should leave with them, as well." His face fell. "But I'll see you tomorrow night?" It was a question, not a statement. I knew he'd just declared his *like* for me, but I wanted to be sure he meant it and wasn't only keeping me on the line as a back-up. Back-up for what, I had no idea. But then again, all of the thoughts which ran through my mind didn't make a lick of sense.

He reached for my hand, his eyes quickly shifting to Matt before he leaned in and gave me another kiss. A passionate, lust-filled kiss.

He was marking me. Claiming me in front of the one guy he viewed as a threat.

I sure hope he isn't thinking of throwing me over his shoulder and beating his chest like a caveman.

That would be taking it a little too far.

~15~

Sara

Agreeing to let me use her car, Alexa knew all about the dinner plans I had with Alek. Every time she brought it up, she would wiggle her eyebrows and laugh. It was her not-too-subtle way of letting me know she thought Alek and I would sleep together afterward. I dismissed her antics with nothing but a smile. In reality, I didn't know what would happen. I'd never wanted anyone more, but I also didn't want to be just another notch on his bedpost, especially since I didn't have any of my own.

I was trying not to overthink the upcoming situation, instead focusing on what I was going to wear. I didn't want to go super comfy, but I didn't want to get too dressed up, either. It was supposed to be a casual dinner at his house, or so that was my interpretation from the nonchalant way he'd invited me.

As if reading my thoughts, Alexa barged into my room all excited. After a very long debate, we settled on an outfit we both deemed appropriate. A red, sleeveless top with cream satin edging around the deep V and shoulders was my first and only choice, fitting me to perfection. I paired it with my best pair of dark skinny jeans and my leopard-print heels to kick it up a notch.

Feeling sexy, I made sure to wear my best underwear, a black lace bra and matching thong I'd spent a small fortune on a while back. But I'd never had a reason to wear it before. Again, not saying I knew what would happen, but at least I'd be prepared.

As I was finishing up my hair, Alexa yelled to me from the front room.

"Hey, Sara, a package was delivered for you. It's a small manila envelope, and it feels like there's something small and hard inside. Hurry up so you can open it."

I wasn't two feet in the living room before she shoved the envelope at me.

"Open it, open it. I want to see what it is already," she said, jumping from one foot to the other, her blonde hair bouncing over her shoulders. I had to admit her curiosity and excitement was a little contagious.

I finally tore the top of the envelope off and turned it upside-down. What fell out couldn't possibly be what I'd thought it was, right?

"Holy shit, is that what I think it is?" Alexa asked, staring at the object in my hand.

"It fucking better not be," I bit out, surprise and irritation woven into my tone.

The small, hard object was an Audi key ring, complete with an extra valet key. I didn't even have to ask who it was from.

We were making our way outside to see if it was for real when my phone dinged. It was a text message from Alek. *Of course.*

Don't overthink it, Sara.

I've pre-loaded my address into the navigation system.

Looking forward to seeing you. – Alek

Once we stepped outside, we practically tripped over it. There, in the very first parking space, was a bright red, shiny new Audi. Alexa grabbed the keys from my hand and clicked the unlock button, instantly sliding into the driver's seat. Slowly making my way around to the passenger's side, I opened the door and hesitantly entered the car.

Alexa broke the silence with her usual banter. "What the fuck, Sara? He bought you a car? A brand new Audi? Do you know how much these cars cost? Wow!" Her excitement only fueled my disbelief.

"Obviously, I can't accept the car, Lex. There is no way in hell I'm letting him buy me a car, let alone a brand new one." I think I was trying to convince myself more than Alexa at that point.

"What do you mean you can't accept it? This is probably chump change to him." Her eyes were busy taking in every fancy aspect of the vehicle. "And you *do* need a car, Sara, so why not? He obviously wants you to have it."

I did need a car, but I didn't need *that* car.

"I'll drive it to his house tonight, but I'm leaving it there. I can't accept it. It's too much."

"You're crazy, girl." She laughed, honking the horn and jumping from the noise. "But at least you get to drive it, even if it's only for one night."

Finally, after ten minutes of sitting in a car I was only going to give back, we made our way back inside.

Once I was finished getting ready, I took one last look in the mirror and grabbed the rest of my things before heading toward the front door once again.

"Be careful and have fun, Sara. Seriously, enjoy yourself tonight." She winked and closed the door behind me as I left.

~16~

Sara

Before I set the car in drive, I decided to give him a quick call, letting him know I was leaving and would be a few minutes late.

"Hello, sweetheart. Are you on your way?" he asked, his voice instantly making my body bristle with anticipation.

Sweetheart? I was taken off-guard by the term of endearment. Although I thought it was a bit too soon for him to be referring to me in such a manner, I'd been happy to hear it.

"Uh...yeah. I'm leaving now, so I should be there in about a half hour or so, barring there are no traffic issues. Oh, and by the way, thank you but no thank you." I gave him a brief moment to respond. But there was only silence. "The car is a very generous gift, but I cannot accept it, Alek. I'm only driving it to your place so I can leave it there. I'm not taking it home with me."

He wasted no time. "Nice try, but you're keeping the car, Sara." He was discordant on the other end of the phone. I could tell instantly he was getting aggravated and I didn't want to ruin the upcoming evening, so I didn't push the issue.

"We'll discuss this later. I'll be there soon."

"I will be counting the minutes." His voice was calmer, much more content. Boy, I never knew anyone who could switch tones so quickly. *Moody man.*

The drive to his house was very relaxing. No imposing traffic to speak of. Plus, it didn't hurt the car handled like a dream, a pure pleasure to maneuver. I had the radio on but kept the volume low enough so I could hear the directions.

The female voice announced I'd arrived at my destination. Making the final right turn, I drove up a wide, dark driveway. Just ahead of me was a single security gate. When I'd pulled close enough, I stopped by the box and pressed the call button.

"Hello," a sexy voice called out.

"I'm here."

There was no response, only the sound of the gate starting to open.

It was but a minute before I'd come to the front of his house, a large, circular driveway swallowing up the front section of the home.

The sun had dipped below the horizon, casting a soft glow over the sky, so I wasn't truly able to get a good look at my surroundings. All I could see was a huge, red-brick house, the color of it almost seeming old-worldly.

I turned off the engine and flipped down the visor to get one last look at myself. Before I could grab the handle, my car door opened and I was greeted by the man I'd come to see. He extended his hand, welcoming me to exit the vehicle. His touch was warm, immediately putting me at ease.

"Good evening, Sara. Thank you so much for coming." His voice always did strange things to me. "I hope you found the house without much difficulty."

"Hello." I flushed, naughty images already racing through my head. "Yes, I found the house with ease, but it was mainly due to the navigation system," I added.

He simply smiled. "This way," he said as he ushered me toward the front door, his hand resting on the small of my back the entire time.

The entryway looked to have been at least fifteen-feet tall, the big mahogany door encased by etched glass all around the framing. Although beautiful to look at, I thought it wasn't very private. Anyone could see into the foyer, the carved glass only slightly distorting the view. *But I guess that's what the security gate is for.*

My eyes roamed all around as we entered, trying my best to take in as much as I could. But for as beautiful as his home was, I'd envisioned something completely different.

Had I thought he lived in some sort of mansion? Maybe.

Had I thought his house was going to be a mixture of homey and sophisticated? For some reason, no.

As he ushered me in further, I took notice of a huge chandelier hanging directly over a center table, an arrangement of flowers which would surely make Katherine proud sitting directly on top.

Looking down, I saw a gorgeous, cream-colored marble which welcomed my every footstep.

Elegant and beautiful, much like the owner of the house.

"Sara?" he called out when I'd stopped moving altogether.

"Sorry, I was just taking in the view." He merely smiled again and gestured toward a room which was off to the left of the main entrance.

"Please, make yourself at home. I'll be right back. I want to check on dinner."

After he left, I was really able to admire the room. It appeared to be a formal sitting area. A huge fireplace, meant to be the focal point, called to me as soon as I entered. Detailed stone impressions surrounded the entire piece of artwork. It was breathtaking.

In the midst of my fascination, he had snuck up behind me, the hairs on the back of my neck standing up when I felt his breath on my skin.

"Sorry to keep you waiting. Please, forgive me," he said as he kissed my neck.

I turned around slowly, taking my time before actually looking at him. I needed those extra seconds to try to compose myself. Once my eyes locked on his, I felt my heart skip a beat. Maybe two. Yes, I'd seen him outside when he came to greet me, but it was dark. There, in the light of his house, I could see how truly stunning he was. The soft burnt-orange sweater he was wearing set off his devastatingly green eyes and thick, dark hair. As I glanced him over from head to toe, I noticed he was wearing jeans, which immediately put me at ease. Even though his clothes probably cost more than I made in a month, the casual attire comforted me. Weird, I knew, but it did.

It was then I noticed his eyes mimicking my own, roaming possessively all over me. An undeniable heat poured from his look, one which needed to be tamped down immediately if we were ever going to make it to dinner.

"Wow. Every time I look at you, I can't quite get over how beautiful you are." He walked toward me, his tongue parting his mouth and slowly running over his bottom lip.

Encroaching on my personal space, he eventually stopped when the front of his boots hit my shoes. He reached out and hooked a finger under my chin, coaxing my face upward until we were staring into each other's eyes. Without a single word, he leaned down and pressed his lips to mine, his warm breath tickling my mouth. It was a soft kiss, but it was as sensual as ever. He finally pulled back, making me stumble forward a step.

"I'm not starting something I won't be able to control, especially before I get a chance to feed you." He consistently seemed pleased with himself whenever he realized he rendered me a pool of desire.

I was disappointed to say the least. I wanted to be consumed by the man every time I came in contact with him.

It couldn't be healthy. Not on any level.

"Come now, dinner is almost ready," he said as he took my hand and led me toward what I assumed was the kitchen.

My eyes continued to dart everywhere. "You have a beautiful home, Alek," I offered, the smile of awe never leaving my face.

"Thank you. I've put a lot of hard work into this place. I helped design it from the ground up. Even had a major hand in decorating it. I'm very pleased with how it all turned out." He grinned as he quickly looked around his masterpiece.

His smile was one of the many things about him which enticed me. Forget about when his dimple decided to make an appearance. At that point, I was reduced to nothing but a horny woman.

Trying my best to rein in my overactive hormones, I decided to find out a bit more information. "How long have you lived here?" I asked, still gripping his hand.

"I've been here about five years now." He suddenly took on a faraway look, as if he was in deep thought. "I plan on being here for quite some time."

Okay...

Time to gather some more info.

"Do you have staff who work here?" I wasn't quite sure why I'd even asked him that question.

"I have someone who comes in twice a week to clean, but that's about it. Why? Should I have a live-in maid, butler, groundskeeper?" he asked.

I suddenly became uncomfortable. "Uh...no...I..." I stammered.

"You are too easy to rile up, Sara. I'm only teasing you."

With my free hand, I lightly smacked him on the arm. "Don't do that. I never know when you're serious."

He halted all movement and turned to face me. "Oh, you'll know when I'm serious," he all but growled as he pushed me backward until my back hit the wall. Hovering his lips above mine, he softly spoke, his breath tickling my mouth. "I've made Coq au Vin. I hope you like it."

He said nothing else.

He didn't move.

He was teasing me.

Tempting me.

I closed my eyes, all too enthralled with the man who was sweetly torturing me.

All of a sudden, he gifted me with a quick kiss before pulling me onward toward our destination.

What the hell was that?

We finally reached the kitchen and I was speechless yet again. All of the top-of-the-line appliances were scattered throughout. Every convenience one could ever want. There were a few items I didn't quite recognize, not that I was schooled in such expensive things.

My curiosity took over. I approached one such appliance and ran my hand over it, willing it to perform for me.

"What is this used for?"

He furrowed his brow and tilted his head. Clearly, my ignorance was shocking. "It's a bread maker. I like to make fresh bread every couple days." His lips curved upward, seemingly amused by my every question.

"The only bread I buy comes already sliced and in individual plastic sleeves." *Smooth, Sara.*

"I'll make sure you get your own fresh batch to take home with you then. You really don't know what you're missing, babe."

There it is again. Another term of endearment. I could definitely get used to being addressed in such a manner, but it was still throwing me off.

As if sensing my sudden disconnect, he continued talking. "You'll never want to eat store-bought bread again. You'll see."

We eventually ended up in a formal dining room, a table so huge it took up the entire center of the space. *I hope he doesn't expect us to sit at opposite ends.* My need to be close to him was always too much.

Deciding to check out the piece of furniture, I walked all around it, noticing there were already two place settings situated right next to one another. *Thank goodness.*

"This is a beautiful table. Where did you find something so large?"

His back straightened and his head was held high, obviously very proud of his possession. "I had it crafted in Italy and shipped here. I was wandering through a local craftsman's shop when I was there on business last year and really liked his work, so I commissioned him to make this piece for me. I'm extremely pleased with it," he said, running his hand over the back of one of the intricate chairs. "Look at the etched detailing he did up each of the legs and all around the edge of the table. He's a true artist."

"It really is quite breathtaking."

As I made my way around the rest of the table, admiring it in its entirety, I noticed even the dinnerware seemed quite expensive.

Sensing my quick reservation, he made his way in my direction. "Are you all right, Sara?"

"Yeah, I'm okay. It's just...I kind of feel out of my element here, Alek. Everything is so over-the-top, fancy and sophisticated, and I'm ...me. Simple."

"You are anything but simple, my dear."

I couldn't help myself, the verbal spewing too much to hold back. "Why do you keep referring to me in such ways?" I needed to know if he talked to every woman with such sincerity and unabashed affection.

"What do you mean exactly?" I could tell I'd thrown him for a loop with my sudden off-the-wall question.

"You keep calling me sweetheart and babe."

"Do those names make you uncomfortable? Do you *not* want me to call you those things?" He seemed perplexed—at my oddness, I was sure.

"It's not that I don't like to hear them. It's just...they seem like names you would call your girlfriend, or wife."

"While I'm not quite ready to propose yet," he laughed, "Would you be more comfortable with the terms of endearment if you were my girlfriend? If it's something you'd like, I could definitely do that."

Wait...what? Where the hell did that come from? Is he serious? I looked around to see if there was someone else in the room with us he could be talking to. *Is this a joke?*

"Well?" He breached the small space between us, reaching out and pulling me into him. He stared at me, but all I could do was avert my gaze, not sure what to think.

"Sara, look at me." I heard only demand in his tone.

When I finally connected with those dreamy eyes of his, I almost faltered. "What?"

"Do you want this relationship to be exclusive? If so, I could easily comply, and gladly, I might add." *There is that damn smile of his.*

I didn't know Alek enough yet to know whether or not he actually wanted what he was proposing. From my small amount of research on the man, he didn't do the girlfriend thing. *But what the hell do I know? It's just all magazine rumor trash anyway, right?*

"Are you going to give me an answer anytime soon? It's not a trick question, love. I promise."

Go big or go home, right? "Do you want to be exclusive with *me*, Alek? I mean really exclusive, as in no other women, at all?"

"I'm fully aware of what exclusive means, Sara. Do you? It also means no flirting or touching any other man. Is that something you can accommodate?" *Is he serious?*

"You make it sound like I hang all over strange men, flirting endlessly with them. But I don't behave like that. Not at all. I'm pretty reserved with that type of stuff."

"What about the way you are with Matt? You seem pretty friendly with him." His demeanor started to change, his grip on me tightening, pulling me that much closer.

"Really? Do I have to go over this again?" I asked, beyond frustrated he wouldn't let the issue with Matt go. "Besides, he's my friend and I feel comfortable around him, so he's someone I'm affectionate with, whether it be hugging or kissing." I could see the look on his face becoming harsher, going from semi-relaxed to instant fury.

"You kiss him?" he practically shouted, his nostrils widening, air sucked through his teeth in haste.

"On the cheek, Alek!" I shouted back. "I don't make it a habit going around making out with my friends."

"Oh." As if contemplating his next question, he waited a few seconds before opening his mouth again. "Did he ever actually tell you he was gay, or are you just assuming he is?"

"He never came out and told me, per se, but I see the way he looks at other men when we're out together. Those looks, mixed with the fact he's never with a woman, only lead me to the ultimate conclusion. I think he came close once to blurting it out, but I guess he lost his nerve."

I suddenly stiffened in his embrace, our conversation making me feel as if I was betraying my friend on some level.

"I still don't like it. I won't be comfortable with you hanging around him until I know for sure he doesn't want to fuck you."

"Alek!" I exclaimed. "Really? Come on. Now you're just being ridiculous and unreasonable. I'm not going to stop hanging out with Matt because you think he wants me. I'm telling you, it's the farthest thing from the truth."

His ludicrous statement had me trying to free myself from his hold. I sure as hell wasn't going to be controlled by someone because they had certain thoughts about certain things.

"Where are you going? Why are you trying to get away from me?"

"I won't let anyone tell me who I can and can't be friends with or hang out with. That is a definite deal-breaker for me, Alek. I won't be controlled by anyone." My voice rose an octave with each statement.

"That's not what I'm trying to do, sweetheart," he stated, his demeanor softening a little bit. "I only want to protect you and make sure you're safe, and if it means asking you to refrain from acting in a certain way, then so be it. I want you to live your life the way you want to, but with some adjustments which will put my mind at ease...where your safety is concerned. So, if you tell me you truly feel Matt is gay, well, then I'll trust your judgment on the issue. But no touching or flirting with any other man. Can we at least agree on that?"

I certainly didn't understand his overwhelming need to protect me. He'd said as much on numerous occasions. But I guess it wasn't the worst thing, although I already knew he'd be using it as an excuse going forward, something we'd surely battle over.

"Deal," I responded. Really, it was a no-brainer. Why would I ever entertain another man when I had him in my life? I would have to be certifiable.

He seemed to appreciate my agreement, leaning down to plant a kiss on my mouth. As with every other intimate encounter, I was instantly turned on, wanting him to continue his lovely display of affection.

But it wasn't to be. He drew back and said, "There. It's settled then. We're exclusive."

I was still a bit confused by the turn of events. Never did I expect him to propose exclusivity so soon, if at all. It could all be over within a week, or a month. I was praying that wasn't the case, but the simple truth was I just didn't know.

The only thing I could do was sit back and enjoy the ride.

~17~

Alek

All throughout dinner, I knew there was something on Sara's mind, something she was holding her tongue about until the meal was finished. Thinking it could only be one thing, I braced myself and prepared my argument. We both knew I was going to win out. I just had to make her see it from my point of view. Again.

Truth be told, I was actually looking forward to the back and forth of it. People constantly agreeing with me was rather boring. I needed a challenge, and Sara would most certainly give me what I craved.

"Alek," she started. *Here we go.* "I want to have a serious conversation with you, and I don't want you to dismiss anything before I've had my say." She looked nervous, avoiding eye contact with me for the most part.

"Sara," I called out. She stopped looking down at her hands and locked eyes with me. "I think I already know what this is about, but I promise to let you have your say before I present my side of things. This should be good, so go ahead, give it your best shot." I laughed before taking a sip of my drink.

Her back straightened before she spoke, strength evident in her posture. "I can't accept the car." I opened my mouth but remembered I'd told her she could finish her argument first. Snapping my lips shut, I nodded, allowing her to continue.

"While I appreciate the *very* generous gift, I simply cannot accept it. It's too expensive, and we've only known each other a short time. It's too impulsive and extravagant. So...while I thank you again for the gesture, I'll be leaving it here tonight, with you. I'm sure you'll be able to return the car easily enough." She took a big inhale of air before continuing. "I've been taking care of myself for a long time, and it makes me uncomfortable to have things given to me. It just isn't my way. In addition, I don't want you to feel like you should buy me things because you have the resources. I don't want your money. I like you for you, simple as that."

Leaning forward on the table, I came as close to her as I could while still giving her space. Her defenses were up, and she was probably going to lose her shit when I responded. *Oh, well. She'll have to get over it.*

"Are you done? Did you say everything you wanted to? Because now I'll say my peace and it will be final." I made sure I had her full attention before speaking again. "While I appreciate your speech...you're keeping the car."

The last syllable didn't even leave my lips before I rose from the table and started clearing it, grabbing her dishes first.

Plus, I wanted to get rid of any weapons she had in front of her. Just in case.

I dared not look in her direction, knowing full well she was upset. I didn't say what I did to rile her up. I said it because it was the truth. No way was I going to let her flit around with no vehicle.

"You're not serious, are you? Tell me you're kidding, Alek!" She had risen from the table as well, bracing herself behind her chair for support. "You're not going to dismiss me with a simple *what I say goes* type of attitude. Because that sure as hell isn't me, either. So, how about this? You can shove the car right up—"

I cut her off before she got a chance to finish.

"Hold up. Don't get so damn testy about this. It isn't that big a deal, so can you please calm down?"

"Well, if it's not a big deal then you won't mind taking it back."

"You're going to keep the damn vehicle and here's why. I worry about you when I'm not with you, and if I can gift you something you actually need and will put my mind at ease, well then, that's exactly what I'm going to do. You don't have any form of transportation, and I don't like the thought of you waiting alone for a ride or taking the bus with a bunch of strangers. And while we are on the subject, you are now my girlfriend and as your man, I will be showering you with many presents, so get used to it. You can fight me on every one, but just know I'll always get my way. Like I won out with the security system issue, I *will* win this one, as well. You'll find I will *always* win when it comes to keeping you safe, Sara."

I saw the reservation on her face. She was calmer than she was before I'd started my spiel, but I wasn't sure yet if she still had some fight left in her. I almost bent her over the table when she told me to shove the car, my excitement pressing tight against the zipper of my jeans.

"Fine. I'll keep the car. *For now.* When I can afford to buy my own, which will now be in the near future, you'll take this one back. Agreed?" She looked at me with expectant eyes.

"Agreed. Can we move on now?"

After all of the dishes had been cleared, I offered to give her a tour of my home.

I couldn't help but be amused over every little thing she found fascinating. I watched her. Closely. Her mouth would fall open when she found something intriguing, whether it was a painting on the wall or a simple gadget. When she was confused, mainly over the main remote I used to operate the TV, sound system and lighting, she would bite her lip, her brow knit in wonderment.

It took every ounce of control to keep my hands to myself, especially when we entered my room. I kept glancing at my bed, wishing for nothing more than to pick her up caveman-style, carry her over and throw her on top of it. I imagined ripping her clothes from her body as my mouth tasted every inch of her flesh, my fingers making good work of revving her up to take me fully.

"Don't you get lonely here all by yourself?" she asked, pulling me from my horny thoughts.

"To be honest, I don't spend much time here. I travel a lot for work, so I stay at some of my other homes, probably as much as I stay here."

"Uh...your *other* homes? How many do you have?" *There's that uncomfortable look again.*

"I have five other homes. Well, three actual houses, one apartment and a suite in one of my hotels. They're spread out all over the country. It makes it easier for me when I have to travel from place to place."

I knew something was bothering her, and I knew what it was without probing too much. I needed to resolve this once and for all. Halting any further movement, I turned her around and pulled her near, my hands gripping her arms to keep her close.

"Does my wealth bother you? You can tell me."

"Well, if I'm being honest...it does a little bit. I'm very happy for you that you're so successful, really I am. But I don't fit into this world, and unfortunately, you're going to see it, too, sooner or later."

"You fit into my world because you're with me, Sara. Simple as that." I didn't know what else to say except the truth.

At a loss for words, she shrugged off my hold and made her way toward the bed. I couldn't help it; my eyes were glued to her ass. I had to remember to tell her how much I appreciated those damn jeans. The sway of her hips was entrancing, making my cock twitch to life. I knew what I wanted to happen between us, but I wasn't so sure she was game yet. And I wouldn't push the issue if she wasn't ready. We had all the time in the world.

"Let me guess, you bought your bed from Italy?" she asked as she ran her fingers over one of the four wooden posts. *Oh, how I would love to feel those fingers wrapped around my...*

"Alek?" she called. *Shit, yeah, she did just ask me a question.*

"Sorry. Yeah, I did. The same artist who made the dining table constructed this piece for me, as well. He actually made all of the furniture you see in here. Do you like it?"

All she could do was nod in response.

I hadn't even realized I was walking in circles around her, probably making her a little wary. I'd been told I was quite intimidating at times. Hopefully that wasn't how she felt. Either way, she moved away from me to inspect the rest of my bedroom, my eyes following her every movement. Every time she caught me looking at her, she would sheepishly smile and turn away.

My overwhelming need to touch her became too much. Enough was enough. Without wasting another second, I walked up behind her as she was checking out one of the paintings on my wall.

Her scent enveloped me as I leaned in close, moving her long hair to the side. Her breath hitched when she felt my lips on her neck.

"What do you want to do, Sara?"

I envisioned us in all sorts of compromising positions, really hoping it would be the night she gave herself to me. Surely she was nervous, so I had to take things slow—if it was what she wanted, of course.

Her head fell back against my shoulder as I nibbled at her sensitive flesh.

"Sara? What do you want to do?" I repeated, the rasp in my voice surprising even me.

"Anything you want." *Well, it looks like she gave me the answer I was hoping for.* But I needed to make sure she was serious.

"Turn around," I demanded.

When our gazes met, I saw it. I'd witnessed the desire in her honey-colored eyes, her pupils dilated in her excitement.

As I was about to ask her a question, she reached up and pressed her mouth against mine, her warm tongue teasing my lips. *I'm gonna lose it if she keeps doing that.*

She backed away for a split-second, put her hands on my chest and repeated her glorious statement from moments before. "Anything you want, Alek."

"You know what I'm taking that as, don't you? Do you know what you're telling me, Sara?"

Breathlessly, she whispered, "Yes."

Oh, to hell with it. I was done talking. I crashed my hungry mouth against hers, snaking my arms around her to pull her close again. Her luscious lips parted, allowing me the entrance I was so hungry for.

She tasted sweet.

She tasted forbidden.

Before things progressed too quickly, I wanted to get *the talk* out of the way. It was simply necessary.

I broke free from our kiss and took a quick step backward, looking into her eyes the whole time.

"What?" she asked.

"Are you on the pill? Are you protected?"

"No," she answered, a light blush creeping over her cheeks. I was sure she hadn't had this conversation with anyone before—at least that was what I was telling myself, not wanting to picture another man's hands all over her.

"Oh. It's okay," I said, a little disappointed. While I'd planned on using a condom anyway, the mere thought of taking her bare excited me. I knew she was clean, being a virgin and all, but so was I. Regular testing proved so. Plus, the fact I'd always used protection in the past, some women often having an agenda of snagging rich men. Hell, I'd even heard horror stories of some trying to blackmail men of my wealth.

Having said and asked what I needed, I pushed all thoughts aside to focus on the vision before me. *No more time for thinking.*

"Take off your clothes, Sara."

Her eyes widened but she complied. Kicking off her shoes, she made quick work relieving her body from the fabric which covered it. Her movements mesmerized me. The elongation of her arms as she pulled her shirt over her head was a dance, her limbs stretching and swaying as the material danced over her skin. Every bend of her body entranced me. She turned her back to me, her fingers playing in the waistband of her jeans. With a soft turn of her head she watched as she shimmied the material over her hipbones, cascading seductively over the plump curve of her ass. Bending forward, she pulled them the rest of the way down, kicking them to the side as if they offended her.

Turning back around, she stood before me in nothing but her bra and panties. My heart beat faster, my breaths coming so quickly they almost escaped me completely.

"Fuck, baby. You're perfect."

She dipped her head, clearly not completely comfortable with my compliment. After a few seconds, she looked up again, resolve set firm in her stare. "Are you going to take off your clothes, or are you going to leave me out here hanging by myself?" she joked, although the look in her eyes was nothing to laugh at. She licked her lips in nervousness and it was quite endearing. Hot...but endearing.

I didn't want her to be any more nervous than she already was, so I grabbed my shirt by the neck and pulled it over my head, tossing it to the side before unbuttoning my jeans. Kicking off my own shoes, I worked the fabric down my muscular thighs before kicking them to the side, as well. Her eyes hungrily drank me in, the sight of me causing her to blush again. The color wrapped itself around her entire chest before it crept up her neck and splayed across her face.

It was the most beautiful sight.

Crushing the last few inches of space between us, I reached behind her and unhooked her bra, the material coming away from her chest with ease. Her breasts were on full display and they were all for me. They were round and heavy but very perky, her nipples a dusty pink, pebbled in arousal. Before I could stop myself, my fingers caressed the hardened peaks, pinching the taut skin and making her moan out in pleasure.

When she exhaled a rush of air, I intensified my grasp, eliciting another moan from her perfect mouth. There was simply no more holding back. My fingers made quick work of summoning her excitement as I walked her backward.

"Lay on the bed," I commanded, the roughness in my tone surprising me.

I had to admit, I loved being able to tell her what to do inside the bedroom. And the fact she complied so readily only encouraged me further. *At least she listens to me in here.*

When she laid on her back, I'd taken a few deep breaths to try and calm down. The sight of her lying there before me was almost too much. I'd dreamed of this for so long it was taking extra time to compute it was actually real. Not wanting to waste another precious moment, though, I hooked my fingers in the top of her panties and slowly dragged them down her toned legs, flinging them somewhere across the room to join our other abandoned clothing.

She was completely and utterly bare, her pussy shaved but for a small strip of hair. *What do they call that? A landing strip?* Crawling up the bed, I lowered myself down on top of her, leaning in close so I could taste her lips again. Her body was on fire underneath me, her skin so unbelievably soft to the touch. My hand entwined in the strands of her hair, pulling in my excitement. I was afraid I was hurting her, but the only reaction she gave me was a moan, each and every time I tugged.

Her sounds teased me, drove me wild until I couldn't take it anymore. I broke our kiss and headed south, lavishing her skin with my hungry tongue. She tasted of anticipation, her hands gripping my shoulders the further down her body I ventured.

"Alek," she cried out, a bit of self-consciousness laced around my name. I knew she was a virgin, but I wondered if she'd ever let a guy go down on her before. The instant image had me seeing red, even though I knew I was being irrational. None of my emotions made any sense when I was near her, my brain and heart twisted up until confusion was the only thing I'd felt.

Pushing those crazy thoughts from my head, I focused back on the woman lying beneath me.

"I want to taste you." As the words left my mouth, I saw her instantly relax. "And I am a very hungry man, sweetheart. Your sweet pussy"—I grinned—"is the only nourishment I need." My hands spread her thighs wide. I didn't give her a chance to respond before my tongue shot out and licked her sweetness. She bucked under my assault, so much so I had to put my hand on her hip to keep her still. I smiled as I continued to torment her, her juices coating my greedy tongue. When I dipped inside, I thought she was really going to lose it, her body trembling with excitement.

After a few short minutes, I could tell she was close. Her breathing had become erratic, her hips doing a wonderful job of pumping against my mouth. She was as greedy as I was. Untold pleasure was within her grasp, and she was doing everything she could to claim it. Flattening out my tongue, I licked her one more time before closing my lips around her clit, driving two fingers inside her tight heat. I curved them, flicking against the bundle of nerves just within my reach.

Her screams were like music to my ears. "Alek! I'm coming. Oh, God! Yeeessss!" She gripped my hair tightly in the throes of her passion. It was like lighting a fire within me. A deep moan of my own escaped, mixing with her delicious sounds.

"That's it, baby. Come for me," I coaxed. I never relented, not until I knew she had fully enjoyed every bit of her orgasm. When her grip on my hair loosened, I knew she was coming back down.

Since she was satisfied, it was time for me to join with her. I made my way back up her body, taking each one of her beautiful breasts into my mouth. I loved every inch of this woman. I couldn't believe it had taken me so long to make her mine. *Everything in due time, right?*

Once our mouths connected again, I had to hold myself back from thrusting inside her until I knew she was ready. She was physically ready, I'd made sure of it, but was she emotionally ready? That was what I had to find out.

My cock danced near her entrance, but again I wouldn't do anything until she was sure.

"Are you positive you're ready for this, Sara?" I asked as I gazed into her beautiful eyes. "There will be a certain amount of pain, due to your inexperience, but I'll try to be as gentle as I can." I battled with myself. I wanted nothing more than to surge forward and bury myself to the hilt, her very tight walls gripping me until I could barely move. But I knew I'd never do that—not until she was used to us having sex, at least. No, I would let her dictate what happened. I would follow her lead.

Her gaze broke away from mine and made their way down toward my arousal. Her eyes widened in—what was that? Disbelief?

"Alek, you're not going to fit," she whispered.

I couldn't help it as laughter erupted before I could stop it.

I explained my little outburst.

"You just gave me the biggest compliment. Thank you." When I sensed I needed to be more serious, her uneasiness holding on tight, I tried to reassure her. I leaned down and gave her a loving kiss. "We were made for each other, sweetheart. We were made to fit."

I guess my words were all she needed to hear to abate her worry because the next words out of her mouth just about undid me. "I want you, Alek. I *need* you inside me. I've never wanted anything more in my entire life." Her eyes bore into mine, searching for what, I wasn't sure. But I would do my very best to give it to her.

"Even though we were made to fit together, you're still new to this, so please tell me to stop if it's too much. Promise me you will tell me if you can't continue." There was no response from her except a small thrust of her hips toward me. She was going to make me lose all control if she kept that shit up. "Promise me, Sara," I demanded.

"Yes, I'll tell you if it's too much. I promise." *Why do I not believe her?*

I positioned myself between her thighs, pushing them further apart. Reaching down, I ran my finger through her wet folds to make sure she was still good and ready for me to take her. She was so worked up, was there really any doubt?

"You're ready, baby," I said worshipfully. I ran my tongue across my teeth, preparing myself to devour the woman who had turned my world upside-down.

"Please. I can't take it anymore," she pleaded, arching her back to entice me further. Little did she know, or maybe she *was* aware, she was teasing me beyond what should have been allowable. I was barely holding on as it was.

"Patience, Sara...patience."

If she's going to torment me, then she better be prepared for me to do the same. I was going to torture her until she shamelessly begged for my cock. My fingers were still exploring her sweet pussy, the salacious sounds coming from her tempting mouth only spurring my onslaught further. Rubbing her clit with my thumb, I slowly inserted a finger inside her. A groan escaped her lips once more as I artfully stroked her. My mouth consumed hers, our tongues dueling as if they were performing an age-old practiced dance.

Coming up for some air, I spewed words at her faster than I could think to filter them. But that was what she did to me. She made me lose all sense of myself. "Do you know what you do to me, Sara? You drive me crazy, in every sense of the word. I can't think straight when I'm near you. And now...now, it's taking every ounce of self-control not to tie you up and ravage you until you beg me to stop."

Her expression told me nothing until a sly smile tipped her lips upward.

"Will you fuck me already?" Her brazenness was certainly a surprise, and I loved I was the one who brought it out in her.

Her fingers raked up and down my back, trying to grip me closer, enticing me to push inside her.

Well, goddamn it. It worked. *So much for having her beg.*

"Okay, love. I'll give you exactly what you need," I promised as I reached over and grabbed a condom from the bedside table. After I was covered, I gripped my thickness and lined up against her sex, pushing inside her very slowly. She was so tight it almost hurt. Almost. For the first time in my life, I actually wished I wasn't as endowed as I was, the mere thought of hurting Sara too much. But there was nothing I could do about it so I made sure to take my time with her, pushing inside inch by painstaking inch.

When I was halfway in, her body tensed, immediately halting my intrusion.

Seeing the utter look of concern on my face, she halfheartedly smiled, brought her legs up and wrapped them around my waist, opening herself up a little more for me. Even though it helped, I knew she was still in pain and there wasn't a thing I could do to take it away. Not until I was fully inside, at least.

"I'm sorry, baby, but this is going to hurt, if only for a few seconds. I can't do anything about it." I felt like shit knowing I was the one who was going to be inflicting the pain, but it was necessary to move forward.

Like ripping off a Band-Aid, I thrust forward until we were fully joined. If I hadn't been lying on top of her she would have shot right off the damn bed. But I was pinning her down, so she had nowhere to go.

Her body tightened, her hands pawing at my hips as if she was trying to push me off her. But she never said a word. Only a single tear escaped, breaking me in two at seeing her distress coating her cheek.

My heart beat wildly inside my chest. I thought for sure she would have heard it, but her eyes never gave way to noticing anything other than her own unfortunate discomfort.

I made sure not to move too quickly, giving her enough time to accommodate me. Plus, if I'd started right away, I would've been done in no time at all.

"You are so unbelievably tight," I said through controlled breaths. "I don't want to embarrass myself, so I'm going to go slow for now."

After I reasoned enough time had passed, I started to move, inviting her to find her own rhythm the more comfortable she became. Her initial shock at my intrusion was gone, her back arching and the heels of her feet pressing into the backs of my thighs, silently encouraging me to quicken my pace. I rotated my hips, around and around. As she would match my rhythm, I'd switch it up, making sure our joining would last as long as possible.

Mid-thrust, I asked, "Are you okay? Does it still hurt?" She didn't answer me right away, instead driving her nails into the hot skin of my back. "Sara," I warned. When she still didn't respond, I stopped altogether. Her frown told me everything. "Answer me or I'll stop right now." She remained silent, calling my bluff. As I started to withdraw from her body, she dug her heels harder into my thighs.

"Yes, Alek. I'm fine," she groaned.

Well, that's a shot to my ego if ever there was one.

"You're *fine*?" I asked, a look of displeasure obvious on my scrunched-up face.

"Yeah. Why? What's the problem?"

She had no idea what she'd said. I was going to change that *fine* to a *spectacular*. The big guy down below demanded it. Leaning closer, I buried my face in her neck, nipping and tasting her salty skin. "How about this?" I asked as I reached down and gripped her ass, pushing her further into me. Thrust. Rotate. Thrust. Withdraw halfway. Thrust again. Her low screams told me she loved it. "Are you still *fine*?"

Understanding was written all over her face, a sly smile surfacing as she bit her lip. Her eyes were hooded, desire evident in every look she gave me. I didn't need her to answer me; I knew I'd made my point.

Increasing my speed, I needed her submission. "You're mine now,

Sara. Tell me you're mine," I grunted. My breathing became harsh and ragged, my heart threating to detonate into a million pieces. Her writhing body beneath me only spurred me further, the sounds she made driving me mad. I wanted nothing more than to devour her, so in a rush of ecstasy, I latched on to her heavy breast, gently biting her nipple until it hardened in my mouth.

"Tell me," I repeated, ravaging her mouth next.

"I'm yours, Alek. Only yours." Five glorious words was all it took to push me toward finishing.

"Are you close, baby? I can't hold off much longer." I needed her to come again, and I was doing my best to make sure she did.

"Yes, so close." She closed her eyes and matched my rhythm once again, bringing her quickly to her own release.

"Look at me, Sara. I want to watch as you come on my cock. I want to feel you pulsate and unravel around me."

Her eyes immediately connected with mine. She tangled her fingers in my hair and as her orgasm ripped through her, she tugged with all her might. A slight sting shot through me, but it was the most delicious pain I'd ever felt.

"I can feel you throbbing around me," I groaned. "I can't take it anymore. I'm gonna come!" I shouted. A few more thrusts and I was releasing myself inside her, her walls coaxing every last bit of pleasure from me.

~ ~ ~ ~

After we both had our breathing under control, we laid there for a few minutes, not moving or saying anything. My heavy limbs were surely squishing the life from her. I withdrew and rolled beside her, wrapping the condom in a tissue and disposing of it in a nearby waste basket.

"Are you okay? Was I too rough?" I was genuinely concerned I'd lost control and had hurt her.

"Not at all. It was more wonderful than I could have ever imagined. Truly, it was."

Needless to say, I was both relieved and pleased with her response. "I can't tell you how happy it makes me you chose me to be your first, Sara. And hopefully your last, if I have anything to say about it." I couldn't help myself; it had to be said.

From the look on her face, she was clearly shocked.

"I'm serious. The thought of any other man touching you drives me insane. I don't even want to think about what I would do. Jealousy is a very new feeling to me. But then again, I've never felt about any other woman the way I feel about you. I hope it doesn't scare you." I was secretly hoping I'd not said too much. Or the wrong thing.

"No, it doesn't scare me, Alek."

A few moments of silence passed before we spoke again, and it was pure torment.

"What's going on in that mind of yours, woman? You look like you're deep in thought." I trailed my fingertips over her firm belly, loving the feel of her naked skin. "I hope you're not regretting what just happened." She didn't answer right away and it made me more than nervous, although she couldn't tell because my face was expressionless.

Thankfully, she put me out of my misery quickly. "No, I don't regret it for one second. How could you think such a thing?" She was staring straight ahead, avoiding eye contact with me for some reason.

"Well, I know how some women get after sex. Confusion sets in as to whether or not they should leave. Or stay."

She whipped her head in my directions so fast, it was almost inhuman. "What the hell? I don't want to listen to how other women react after you've had sex with them." Her eyes lit up in hurt. "Are you trying to piss me off right now?" Folding her arms over her breasts, she turned over on her side, blocking me out completely.

I loved her feistiness. Lightly chuckling, I reached over to pull her closer but she wasn't budging. Moving further away from me, she tried to scoot over toward the other side of the bed.

I caught her hand before she fled.

"Sara, come on. Come here. That's not what I meant at all. I was merely trying to say I've heard sometimes, some women, out there in the universe, feel a certain way after having sex. That's all. You can tell me how you're feeling without having to worry I'll be upset, or put off, or whatever way you think I'm going to be. Fuck, now I'm just rambling."

She took a deep breath before joining me again. Resting her head on my chest did wonders in calming my erratic breathing. I'd thought I'd really fucked up for a second, her reaction a little over-the-top from what I was going for. I wrapped my arm around her and pulled her into me, my free hand playing with the strands of her dark hair.

I felt her smile against my skin, causing me to close my eyes in triumph. We both seemed to exhale at the same time and before we knew it, we'd drifted off into a deep slumber.

~18~

Sara

The next two months passed by in a blur. Alek and I enjoyed each other's company, going out to dinner, even taking in the occasional movie. I'd spent time at his house, and in turn he'd stayed over at my apartment, a feat I was sure made him a bit uncomfortable although he never said a word. His place was much nicer than mine, every amenity under the sun there. Still, he never complained.

Everything was progressing perfectly.

It was the happiest I'd been in a really long time.

One particular evening, we'd made plans to have a late dinner. Alek had recently arrived back into town, and instead of him going home and getting a decent night's sleep, he wanted nothing more than to see me. I was thrilled, anticipating seeing his gorgeous face again. I felt like it'd been forever since I'd been near him, let alone touched him. In reality, it had only been four days.

Four very long, lonely days.

"Are we still on for tonight, babe?" he asked, his sexy voice penetrating my phone. It had been a busy day, and I was really looking forward to having a nice, quiet dinner with my man. Then afterwards, we both knew what was going to happen.

What's the saying? Fuck like bunnies? Well, although the saying wasn't too appealing, it was exactly what we'd been doing. We simply couldn't keep our hands off one another.

"Of course. I'll be closing up in an hour or so. Are you picking me up, or did you want me to meet you there?" I wiped the sweat from my brow. I would have liked to say it was because I was running around like crazy, my body overheating from the exertion, but the simple truth was I had no idea why I was getting hot all of a sudden.

And it wasn't the horny kind of hot, either.

No matter. In a couple short hours, I'll be spending some time with Alek.

"I'll pick you up. You know I don't like you driving by yourself at night."

"I'm not eighty. I can see in the dark." I laughed because he was being irrational. As usual.

"Sara," he warned.

"Fine. I'm only trying to help you out."

"Well, there's no need. I don't mind. Not at all."

After we hung up, I tried my best to finish straightening up so everything would be ready come the morning. But the more time passed, the worse I felt.

Finally, when the day was done and the shop had been closed, I made my way home, feeling as if I was going to pass out during the drive to my apartment.

My hands were clammy and I was finding it difficult to breathe, my stomach flipping around so much I thought I'd have to pull over just so I could rid myself of whatever was inside my belly. My temples started to throb, no doubt indicative of one hell of a headache coming my way.

I'd barely put my key in the door when my cell rang.

"Hello," I whispered. I didn't even have the energy for a more audible response.

"Sara? What's wrong?" Alek asked, panic rising in his voice. "Are you okay?"

"Yes. Well...no. I don't think I can go out tonight," I said, trying my best to breathe through the nausea ripping through me yet again.

"Are you sick?"

Ding. Ding. Ding. He hit the nail on the head. Shit! I haven't felt like this in so long. I forgot how crappy being sick is.

I couldn't even muster enough strength to answer him, my mouth watering the sicker I felt. It was a sure sign I'd be visiting the porcelain God very soon.

I took a few steady breaths to calm myself. It didn't work.

"Don't worry, sweetheart. I'll be there as soon as I can," he offered.

"No, Alek. I don't know what this is yet, and I don't want to get you sick."

There was a pregnant pause before he blurted, "I'll be there in an hour."

Before I could even gather any strength to argue, he hung up.

~19~

Sara

I was trying to envision a healthier me, but I couldn't remember what it was like to *not* feel like this. I knew I was being a baby, but it was specific times like this which made me miss Gram even more than usual. She was always there to take care of me when I didn't feel well, which thankfully wasn't often. She would feed me the necessary medication and then make me her special chicken noodle soup. When I wasn't up for the noodles, she would feed me the broth instead.

My one saving grace was that the following day was Sunday, which meant I didn't have to bother Matt with taking care of the shop. Lots of rest and fluids was definitely what the doctor ordered.

As I made my way toward my bed, not even bothering undressing, I was thankful I had given Alek a key two weeks prior. Because there was no way I would have been able to make it to the door to let him in. The living room wasn't far, but it felt like a hundred miles away.

Staring at the ceiling, I tried to focus on anything but being sick.

But it was impossible. The more I tried to convince myself I was okay, the more my body revolted against me.

I barely made it to the bathroom before my stomach turned on me. I hadn't eaten since seven the night before, so I was surprised there was anything even left in my system to get rid of. I thought I would have felt better afterward, but I didn't. All I could do was lie on the bathroom floor, welcoming its coolness on my damp skin. Thankfully, I'd cleaned the entire room two days ago. But then again, the way I was feeling, I couldn't care less if it wasn't up to par.

I must have passed out, because the next thing I knew I was being lifted and carried back to my room, or at least I thought it was my room. I opened my eyes enough to see Alek tucking me into bed. I curled up once he was finished and drifted off again.

"Sara. Sara, wake up. Come on. You have to drink something or you'll get dehydrated. Come on, baby. Open your eyes for a couple minutes then you can go back to sleep." I tried my best to obey, but it sapped the rest of my energy. I was simply too weak. When I didn't budge, he lightly shook my arm. Groaning from the intrusion, I attempted to turn over, my eyes quickly taking in my surroundings.

"Alek," I whispered. "Where am I?" It wasn't my bedroom, the tan walls giving it away. My room was a pale yellow, the color always lifting my spirits.

"I brought you home with me," he stated simply. "I can't take care of you properly at your place." He was still trying to get me to sit up, a feat easier said than done. "Come on, sweetheart. You have to drink this." Once I was propped up against the pillows he'd arranged for me, I very carefully took the drink from his hands, bringing it to my lips and taking the smallest of sips. It was only water, but I knew I had to be careful; the smallest drop could have my stomach flipping.

After I'd managed to swallow four whole sips, I pushed the cup toward him and scooted down the bed again. I wasn't halfway back into my sleeping position before he jostled me again. "Don't lie back down just yet. Here," he said, placing something in my hand. "Take these."

When I glanced down, I saw he'd put two small pills in my hand. Pushing the glass of water back at me, I didn't even question what he'd given me. I knew it was something to help me feel better, and that was all I cared about.

Not saying a single word, I carefully swallowed the medicine before finally settling back under the covers.

He leaned over and placed a kiss on my forehead before tucking me in. He lingered above me and when I opened my eyes, I saw he was simply looking at me. When his gaze met mine, he smiled serenely before taking a step back. "I'll be back shortly to check on you."

I barely heard his last word before I fell into a blissful sleep.

For once, my dreams were pleasant. Actually, they were more than pleasant. They filled my subconscious with hope, a yearning for a happiness I thought would never exist for me. I knew if he'd been watching me, he would have witnessed a smile on my face as I tossed and turned in his big, comfy bed. I would have also gifted him the sight of my back arching off the bed as the alternate world took hold and thrust me into the most erotic dreams I'd ever had.

Alek being the main attraction.

I was filled with hope and the promise of something wonderful happening between me and the one man who'd flipped my damn world on its ass. I knew it sounded corny, but I'd thought such happiness only existed in movies or in Hallmark cards. Hell, I would have been the first to give someone like me the crooked face, skepticism bleeding forth like a river of disbelief.

Instead of jolting awake like I was used to, I peacefully slipped back into the land of the living. I quietly laid there, listening intently to the sounds around me. A soft *tick tock* from the clock beside me on the nightstand. A faint muffled sound from somewhere else in the house. A TV maybe?

But the greatest sound of all?

Peace.

The room was cloaked in darkness, so I wasn't exactly sure what time it was. The only thing I knew for sure was that my stomach rumbled, desperate for some much needed nourishment. What I'd eaten earlier had only been refunded later on.

Feeling a little better, I mustered enough strength to actually make it to the bathroom to pee, the full glass of water I'd had earlier knocking on my tiny bladder.

As I walked back toward the bed, fatigue taking hold rather quickly, Alek strolled into the room. He looked a little irritated, no doubt because I was up and moving around. *I'm sure he didn't want me ruining his nice comfy sheets, now did he?*

"What are you doing up?"

"I had to use the bathroom," I said, amusement counteracting his annoyance.

"Oh."

"Is that okay? Or are you going to tie me to the bed?"

"If I tie you to the bed, it won't be while you're sick." He advanced a step before stopping himself, a devious look playing on his face. I knew exactly what he'd been thinking, and it made me smile. Gathering his wits again, he stepped closer. "Now, let's get you back into bed."

Pulling back the edge of the blanket, he held it up as I scrambled underneath. I watched as he walked toward the other side of the room, admiring his fine ass as he moved.

Sauntering back toward me, I took notice he had something in his hands. It was a bowl, the billowing steam drawing me right in. The closer he came the more the delicious aroma took hold of me, my stomach making some crazy noises.

He'd made me chicken noodle soup, and although it didn't seem like much it was very touching. A man taking care of his woman, bringing her soup when she was sick...was there anything more sweet?

"You didn't have to go through all that trouble, Alek," I said, all the while grateful he'd made the effort.

"No trouble at all. I'll always take care of you." He sat on the bed next to me, careful not to spill the hot liquid. "Always," he repeated as he brought the spoon to my lips.

I reached out to take it from his hands but he pulled back, knitting his brow in quick confusion. *Oh, Lord, he wants to feed me, too?*

All right. I'll give in. Besides, I honestly didn't think I even had enough strength to do it myself, my body shaking a bit in my still-weakened state.

After I devoured the entire bowl of soup, I situated myself further down the bed, snuggling in for a good night's rest. Feeling guilty I couldn't take care of myself right then, it was quickly abated when I saw the way he looked at me.

A look of pride came over him as I allowed him to take the lead. To be the caretaker. To be the man capable of making his woman feel better.

I fell for him even more that night.

~20~

Sara

It took me three days to feel like myself again. Alek had insisted I stay with him until I was a hundred percent, and for once, I actually listened to him.

Thankfully, Matt had been able to step in and run the shop in my absence. It was the only thing Alek didn't truly appreciate, the fact I was relying on another man to help me out. It grated on his nerves, even though he did his best to hide it from me.

But I saw it.

His jaw would tighten whenever he heard me on the phone with my good friend. But he never said anything. Only reacted. Minutely. He was coming around slowly to the idea of Matt. He would never admit it, but I saw his concern slowly diminish the more time passed.

My last night held willingly captive, we watched movies and ate take-out. I was pretty much back to normal; the only symptom I'd ever been sick was a touch of weakness. Not being able to eat normally for a few days took its toll on me. It was the first time I'd been able to eat solid food in days, the chicken and broccoli the most delicious thing I'd ever tasted.

I'd been feeling so well, I'd tried to convince Alek to let me have my way with him. He didn't budge, though he promised me an all-inclusive tour of Deveraville when I was completely back to normal.

Even though I was disappointed, it gave me something to look forward to. Something to fantasize about and something to build toward.

After we'd watched yet another movie, I'd fallen asleep on his chest, his warmth too inviting not to.

~~~~

A few hours after I'd drifted off, I awoke with a start. One of my nightmares decided to pay me a visit, making sure to scare the living hell out of me, as usual.

The serenity was nice while it lasted, I guess.

Thump. Thump. Thump.

My heart rammed so quickly I felt its pulse through my entire body. I did my best to push away the feeling of terror which had gripped me not minutes earlier. Once I deemed back in control, I turned my head to the side and saw Alek looking at me.

Luckily, he hadn't noticed the light sheen of sweat covering my body, or the terrified look in my eye when I'd first woken.

Turning fully toward him, I focused on his eyes. Or at least, I tried to. He moved away, a look playing on his face as if he wanted to tell me something. As I prepared to ask him about it, he spoke, tearing me from whatever thoughts had plagued me in that moment.

"Are you hungry?" he asked as he reached down and entwined his fingers with mine. Leaning closer, he nuzzled the side of my neck before lavishing my skin with his tongue. "I know I am."

His breath tickled me. I laughed and tried to move away, but his hold on me was persistent. "And what are you hungry for, Alek?" I asked while still squirming, hoping he'd changed his mind about giving me what I'd wanted earlier.

"You, of course." Before I could say another word, he was on top of me, pushing himself between my legs. My heart beat wildly inside my chest, but it wasn't from fear or anxiety. It was from excitement, my need for him too great to contain any longer.

To show him how much I wanted him, I captured his mouth, teasing his lower lip with my tongue until he opened up, which didn't take long at all. I loved the taste of him, his warm breath mixing with mine. The way he made me feel was addictive.

With every kiss and caress he gave me, I felt myself falling for him more and more.

Mind, heart and soul.

"Please," I moaned, gripping his ass with my plea. But what did he do instead of giving me what I wanted? He broke our kiss and climbed off me, walking toward his dresser. Pulling out a pair of pajama bottoms, he threw them on before he approached me again.

"You have no idea how much I would love to fuck you again, baby, but I know enough to realize you're probably still a bit weak. And what I have planned requires a lot of strength and endurance." He reached under the covers and gently ran his finger over my need for him.

I gasped.

He withdrew his hand before I could fully enjoy it. Drawing it up to his mouth, he parted his lips and dipped his finger inside. "Sweet," he teased, winking and walking toward the door. "Since I can't eat what I want right now, I'll settle for a veggie omelet. You want one?" He was halfway through the door before I realized what he'd asked me.

"Yes, please!" I hollered as he disappeared down the hallway.

Damn him.

I glanced over at the clock and noticed it was really late. I didn't normally make it a habit of eating at that time, but I had to admit I was a bit famished, my body on the brink of a full recovery.

I didn't feel like putting my own clothes back on so I made my way into his very large closet, deciding to throw on one of his dress shirts. Reaching forward, I grabbed one off the hanger. Well, I tried to anyway. One side of the shirt was stuck and the more I pulled on it, the more it seemed to want to stay exactly where it was. I reached in further to untangle it, harshly yanking it toward me. Not only did the piece of clothing wedge free, but I'd dislodged something else, as well. I jumped back as something fell to the floor and hit my foot.

Damn it. He's going to think I was snooping. I was curious, of course, but it wasn't right to go through his private things. Bending down, I reached for the fallen object and realized it was a folder, the contents scattered all over the closet floor. They appeared to be photographs, but I couldn't be sure because they were all face-down. Picking everything up as quickly as possible, I noticed something familiar written on the lip of the folder.

It was my name.

Odd.

Taking a deep breath, I tried to push away the sudden uneasy feeling coursing through me. Part of my brain was telling me to throw everything back together without looking. But the other part was urging me to look and not ignore what was staring me in the face.

Of course, my curious side won out.

I quickly reached down and grabbed some of the photos. Still having some reservations, I sucked in a deep breath, counted to three, exhaled and flipped the pictures over so I could get a good look at them.

Trying my best to rationalize what I was looking at, I studied each and every one of them. But there was no explanation. A cloud of confusion engulfed me, threatening to tear the very breath from my body.

All of the items I held in my trembling hands were pictures of *me*. There must have been at least a hundred in total, all taken over the past eight years or so, long before I'd moved to Seattle.

There were some of me coming and going from the house I'd shared with my grandmother; pictures of me at my job at the bookstore I used to work for; pictures of me pumping gas, shopping and even hanging out with friends.

The list went on and on.

There was one picture which really caught my attention. It was of me leaving my therapist's office, looking beat-down and emotionally drained. As my heart picked up speed, something dawned on me. All of these pictures were taken *after* the incident. To be sure, I looked through all of them again, but the conclusion was the same.

None of them were taken before my life had changed forever.

My mind drifted to a time when I was a very carefree and trusting person. I always looked for and believed in the good in people, often ignoring warning signs which should have been obvious to me. Even though I had endured tragedy early on in my life with the loss of my mother, I still lived a pretty sheltered upbringing. I believed everyone had a loving grandmother like I did. I believed everyone was honest, loving, kind and generous, simply because it was how I grew up. I was raised to be kind to others, to help them when they were in need, in any way I could. I lived in a bubble, sheltered from the harshness of the world around me. I used to be thankful I had that kind of naivety, but it ultimately shattered my protected way of life.

A cold chill ran up my spine. I couldn't dwell on the past. I had to forget and move forward...always move forward or he would win. I wouldn't let that happen.

I can't *let that happen.*

I forced my mind to come crashing back to reality.

Why does he have these?

Did he take the pictures? Was he following me the whole time? Did he have someone else following me all those years? I wanted answers. No. I *needed* answers, but I couldn't face him right then.

I had to get the hell out of there.

~21~

Sara

My cell almost slipped from my fingers, I was so shaken. Dialing Alexa's number, I held my breath until she answered. Finally, on the fourth ring I heard her voice.

"Hey, Sara, what's..." I didn't let her finish before I spouted out a barrage of words.

"Alexa, can you please come and get me right now? Please...I have to get out of here." I didn't sound like myself, and I was probably starting to scare her.

"Oh, my God. Sara, are you all right? What happened?" She sounded as panicky as I did.

"I can't get into it over the phone. Please tell me you'll come pick me up." Of course, she agreed. I gave her the address and told her to text me once she reached the end of the road. After that, all I had to figure out was how I was going to get out of there without him noticing. *And how the hell am I going to get the damn security gate open?*

I threw my clothes on, getting dressed faster than I ever had before. There was no time to waste; I had to devise a plan and do it quickly. I debated on whether or not to put the pictures back where I thought they had fallen from or leave them sprawled out on the ground. I ended up leaving them there. That way, he would undeniably know why I'd left.

As I threw on my heels, I heard him coming up the stairs. *Shit!*

"Sara, the food is almost ready. Do you want to come down now?" I could hear him walking down the hallway as he called out to me. *He'll be in the room any minute.* I had to hide, so I went to where everyone eventually tried to shield themselves.

I hid under the bed.

Hopefully, he'll think I'm already on my way down and won't spend too much time up here searching for me.

My breath hitched as I saw his feet come into view. I wanted to desperately close my eyes but I needed to pay attention. I needed to know when he was gone so I could make my escape.

"Sara? Are you in here?" He proceeded to enter the master bathroom, probably assuming that was where I was. But obviously he didn't find me in there.

Once he came upon the mess on the closet floor he stopped.

He didn't move.

He seemed frozen in time, not quite sure what to do.

Then came the cursing, various expletives flying from his mouth so fast it almost didn't sound like English.

Taking off like a bat out of Hell, he ran through all of the upstairs calling out for me. "Sara! Sara, where are you? Please, baby...please, let me explain." His voice disappeared. I could only assume he was running through the downstairs looking for me, as well.

Now's my chance. I had to escape his house immediately. I crawled out from underneath the bed and quietly made my way from his bedroom, peering down the long hallway to make sure he wasn't anywhere to be found.

As quietly as I could, I creeped down the stairwell, being very cautious not to make any noise. I thought I heard him toward the back of the house, near the dining room, but his house was so large I couldn't be sure. I sure as hell wasn't going to stick around long enough to find out.

Before he had the opportunity to find me, I bolted down the rest of the stairs and went straight for the front door. I yanked it open and ran down the steps, heading down the long driveway toward the gate. *Alexa should be arriving soon, so I only have a limited amount of time to try and figure out how to open that damn metal confinement.*

Otherwise, I wouldn't be going anywhere, which was *so* not an option.

A text came through from Alexa as soon as I reached the gate. I didn't text her back, choosing to call her instead.

"Lex, I'm at the gate, but I can't figure out how to get it open!" I yelled, knowing I sounded as frantic as I felt.

"Try to calm down, Sara. See if there's a button somewhere, maybe off to the side of the frame."

I fumbled around in the dark, trying to use the light from my phone to guide me, when I heard Alek screaming my name. I knew he saw the open front door and was coming my way. I had to hurry, or I'd find myself in a situation I wouldn't be able to handle.

Even though I knew he was hiding something big, possibly something dangerous, my heart was having a hard time catching up with my brain. *So the sooner I get out of here, the better.*

"Lex, I can't find it. I can't fucking find it!" When I thought all hope was lost, my finger found a button higher up on the metal frame than where I'd originally been searching. It was hidden behind part of a tree which was hovering over the side of it. The way it was positioned no one would be able to access it from the outside.

Please, let this work...please.

It did. The gate started opening.

My name drifted on the light breeze, goose bumps of fear breaking out all over my body. I could hear Alek getting closer and closer. I pushed my way through the small opening the gate provided, almost getting stuck waiting for it to open wider.

I saw Alexa's headlights down the road so I ran faster than I ever had before, praying I didn't trip over anything in the dark. It wasn't until I'd reached the passenger door did I finally turn around to look behind me. That was when I saw him running down the pathway.

"Sara, please stop! Please, let me explain. It's not what it looks like. Please!" he yelled as he ran toward me.

I had to leave and do it right then before he reached me.

Grabbing the handle, I yanked the door open and jumped inside as if my life depended on it.

"Sara, are..."

I cut her off before she could finish asking if I was okay. "Go, Lex! Go!" She peeled off down the road at my command, not questioning me any further. When I dared to look behind me, I saw Alek in the middle of the road, arms down at his side, looking defeated.

The shrill ring of my phone caused me to jump. I looked down and, of course, it was him calling me. I pressed the ignore button but as soon as it went to voicemail, it started ringing again, and again, and again. Finally, I had to turn it off completely.

"What the hell happened back there? You damn near scared the shit out of me. I thought someone was trying to kill you." She glanced over at me, thinking the worst, I was sure. "What the fuck did he do to you? Tell me."

"Nothing. He didn't do anything *to* me. It was what I found in his closet, by accident. I found pictures of me, probably close to a hundred of them, all taken over the past eight years or so. He has either been stalking me for years or having someone else do it. What I can't figure out is why, Lex. Why?" I asked, as if she was going to have an answer. "Why would he do this? I don't understand." My last rambling was more rhetorical than anything.

Alexa remained silent, probably trying to process everything I'd just dumped in her lap. Hell, *I* was still trying to process it all, and I was the one who was directly involved.

"I guess we never really know people," she said, finally breaking the silence. "If he could fool us, then I guess anyone can."

For some reason, her words were the last straw. I cried. Uncontrollably. I couldn't believe after all this time, I'd finally found the man of my dreams and he turned out to be someone I couldn't trust.

What was the point of it all?

His incessant need to always make sure I was safe seemed odd to me at that point. But if he was following me all those years then he knew how easy it would be for someone else to do it. *Is that why he always wanted to keep me close and out of harm's way? So someone else couldn't do what he was doing?*

My heart broke as I realized I would never find out.

~22~

Alek

My bedroom was in shambles. Everywhere I looked, I saw the destruction I'd caused, beyond enraged to give a shit. I couldn't believe I'd let it come to this. I'd never meant for her to find out the way she did.

I hid it.

I lied about it.

Well, I omitted the truth. Same thing.

How the hell am I going to convince her to trust me now? God knows what's running through her head. But I couldn't really blame her, could I?

As the amber liquid burned its way down my throat, I knew what I had to do.

Convincing Sara to listen to me was going to take work. But I was indeed up to the task.

I'd never give up.

Not until she was mine again.

To be continued in

Shattered...

Coming June 2015

About the Author

S. Nelson grew up with a love of reading and a very active imagination, never putting pen to paper, or fingers to keyboard until a year and a half ago.

When she isn't engrossed in creating one of the many stories rattling around inside her head, she loves to read and travel as much as she can.

She lives in Pennsylvania with her husband and two dogs, enjoying the ever changing seasons.

If you would like to follow or contact her please do so at the follow:

Email Address: snelsonauthor8@gmail.com

Facebook: https://www.facebook.com/pages/S-Nelson/630474467061217?ref=hl

Goodreads: https://www.goodreads.com/author/show/12897502.S_Nelson

Amazon: http://www.amazon.com/S.-Nelson/e/B00T6RIQIQ/ref=ntt_athr_dp_pel_1

Other books by S. Nelson

Stolen Fate

Redemption

Made in the USA
Middletown, DE
11 April 2017